n-Space

Thea Gregory

Copyright © 2025

All rights reserved.

This is a work of fiction. Names, characters, businesses, places, and incidents are either the products of the author's imagination or used in a fictitious manner.

ISBN: 978-1-0693415-1-8

To Martin. I couldn't ask for a better brother, and friend.

Chapter 1

"Are you sure about this, Frida?" The woman's father, Zeke, asked as they entered the spaceport through an airlock that sealed them off from Dome-12's stench. The spaceport was a huge semi-spherical complex, a white blob detracting what must have once been the incredible natural beauty of their planet, Nox-Gamma. Before the humans got to it, anyhow. Zeke squinted as they crossed the threshold, the harsh fluorescent light and reek of artificial cleaners assaulting their senses. Zeke's crow's feet etched inwards and his frown deepened. Frida raised her hand to her nose in a futile attempt to cut the smell. The din of thousands of voices disoriented her. There were humans everywhere, even more than the numbers that crowded the halls of Uni-12 in the central spire of their dome. "I've never been off-world, either," he added, pulling his red luggage behind him. Today he looked all of his 75 years, a circlet of gray hair wrapping around his skull. He had a hawkish nose and full lips. His daughter, Frida, shared the nose but her hair was thick and black, cropped at the jawline. Her wide blue eyes had yet to be graced by age, and she seemed younger than her 27 years. Both were slight and short.

"I'll be fine, Dad," she said, reaching out to take his right hand in hers. "It's just a work thing, not like it's going to be party-central. We're math nerds. Besides, you can have a look around. Explore. Get away from it all for once." She left out the end of the thought: Since you lost mom, all those years ago. That reality hurt too much to put into words. Was it loss for her, or the pain of never having a mother at all that stung more?

They continued through the spaceport, until they came to a wall along the far side. They glanced about, looking for any sign of their ship. They were lucky; most people couldn't leave their home planets unless they were either rich or in the military. Frida didn't know anybody local who had been off-world. She smiled. This was going to be the best time of her life. She could be who she wanted, and grow beyond the reputation that had been given to her back home. They walked along the curved edge, noting every sign. Earth, hell no. Alpha Hyperion. Antares II. Athene. The lists went on and on. The crowd began thinning once they left the passenger loading docks of the populated planets that were known for their still-lush ecosystems and vibrant cultures. Now, Frida and her father were in the area known as the undesirable underbelly of human existence. Still, it wasn't as bad as the front lines, but nothing was as bad as being at the front of an endless war with an alien race who were nothing like us. *Perhaps they know how to treat a planet*, Frida wondered. Wars, destroyed planets, crime, and a pandemic of hopeless youth was all humanity seemed to have going for it.

"Is that it?" her father asked, pointing to a sign in the distance. They were deep into a sea of colorful crates and plain-dressed cargo crew. *This must be the commercial section, the glamorous side of life*, she thought.

Frida squinted, forcing her eyes to focus through the glare of the lights. Elym-One. "That's the place. And our glorious freighter awaits."

"At least it's not a garbage ship," Zeke said, slapping her on the back. "Gotta look at the positives, like I keep telling you."

"Small mercies. You'd think they could spare a small amount from the war fund to invest in academics," Frida said.

"Yeah, but not many people appreciate applied mathematics like you do. They can't comprehend what you see in our world."

Yeah, endless numbers and symbols. The studying. The total lack of romantic interest from other humans, no matter their gender. Such a gift. "Perhaps that's for the best. Though, it will be nice to get away from Nox for a while—see something, maybe breathe real air."

As they approached the port, a few people stood out. One a statuesque woman in blue coveralls with short hair and a perpetual smirk leaned against the door, playing with a phone. Another was scanning bar codes into his manifest, his neat curly hair caressing his ears. The last sat on a box with her legs crossed, juggling a set of three green balls before deftly catching them and setting the cycle going again. A pattern. Frida immediately was drawn to the skill she displayed, the dexterity. Her eyes lighted to the other woman's face. She had freckles and black hair tied in a high ponytail. She was wearing orange coveralls and gazed at the ceiling, as though she did not even need to be aware of her balls to catch them.

"So, this is our ride?" her father asked.

"Yup. This just keeps getting better and better. I hope they're not smuggling." Frida frowned, it was hardly her idea of a good way to travel. What was there to do on this ship? Was it clean? Were the people on board criminals?

"Come on, Frida. Just because they're not in perpetual university doesn't mean they're smugglers."

"And how should I see it?"

"You might see the stars for the first time in your life, how about that for a start? New people, new food, maybe fresh air that doesn't smell of ozone and dust."

"You got me there, Dad." Even more damning, she'd never even seen the moon through the domed city they lived in. Nothing but milky gray, illuminated and dimmed to simulate day and night cycles. With the cycles came noise. With the day, the bustle of a city. With the night, the din of riots and gang fights.

Frida walked up to the tall woman, extending her right hand. "Are you Captain Nin?" she asked, trying to determine how to make eye contact while the woman was absorbed in her phone.

"Yeah, that's me alright. I'm Nin to my crew but you can call me Stari if you like. Are you the Junipers, Frida and Zeke?" Her voice was soft but held a gentle aura of command and control. Nin's black-eyed gaze unsettled Frida, but she steeled herself to it as Nin shook her hand. Frida had been subjected to far worse in school.

"Okay, we're almost ready to go. None too soon, either. I suggest you find a way to stay off-world. Nox is a little too close to the front lines now, if you catch what I'm saying." Nin ran her hand through her hair, pulling herself up to her full height. She dwarfed Frida by almost a head.

"The war is almost half the galaxy away!" Frida's father protested. Everyone knew that.

"Is that what they're saying now on the news?" Captain Nin asked. "Anyhow, not our problem unless you two want to enlist. Neither of you look the type to be fighting the Kijh, no offense."

"No," Frida said, shaking her head, vigorously. "Let's leave the violence to someone else. When can we come on-board?"

Nin gestured to the door. "Juke will show you to your quarters. It's not much to look at but nobody will bother you there. You're welcome to come to the bridge to watch the liftoff, the moon here is a damn good sight from space. One thing, though."

Frida looked up at Nin expectantly as Nin motioned to the woman with the green balls. *Juke, interesting name*, Frida thought.

"Don't mess with my cat. His name is Pesky but he only answers to 'Dumbass.' He's a tabby, can't miss him."

"Got it. Let's get going, Dad." Frida's earlier trepidation had melted away, and she had steeled herself to this mission. She was going to fly far, far away.

Juke walked up to them, built like a willow from the arboretum but with a mischievous glint in her eyes. Her long black hair reflected the steady glow of the dome's light, and her lips twisted into a smile as she eyed Frida. "Guests, eh? Come on in. Don't mind the smell, or the rats. Dumbass isn't doing his job these days." She winked at Frida, motioning them in with a flourish.

"Don't be an idiot, Juke, just get them settled," Nin called over to them. Juke rolled her eyes.

Frida balked. "Rats?" Rats were the bane of the domed cities of Nox—carrying disease and toxicity from the outer world.

Zeke laughed and clapped Frida on the back, giving her a small push. "You wanted adventure, you got it. Let's go. The sooner we get underway and the sooner we get to Elym-One, the better."

Frida followed Juke in, carefully stepping over the threshold into the dark ship. The air shimmered ahead, an otherworldly green that danced with the omnipresent hum of the ship's engines and electronics. "What's that?" Zeke asked, pointing at the aberration.

Juke laughed. "Just decontamination. Nothing to worry about, unless your hobbies include suit-less hiking or skinny dipping."

"If you have done any of that, Frida, you're grounded for life," Zeke said.

She knew he meant it, and people who did that had very short and often painful lives, punctuated by many visits to what passed for a doctor here on Nox. Frida shook her head and stepped into the light. A faint hint of static danced on her exposed skin, a flash of green here or there, and the hint of old air usually only found on the subterranean levels of the Dome. She rubbed her bare arms and walked in, turning to see her father stepping through the detection unit and Juke grinning as she marched through. Frida thought that perhaps familiarity could get her used to the smell, the narrow corridors and flickering lighting, though the latter was a welcome reprieve from the intense light in the spaceport. Her father was right, it all was simply a matter of perspective.

"It's not far. We'll be taking off in about an hour. We have about twenty other distinguished guests on this trip, so get to the bridge early if you want a good view," Juke said as she waved and maneuvered them into a corridor to the right. "Don't worry, I'll have Aesop upload a map of the ship to your phones so you don't get lost."

"Who's Aesop?" Zeke asked.

"That's Nin's name for the computer. It has a reason for everything it does. While we don't always understand, Aesop always gets us through it in the end. Thankfully, it can't navigate the ship on its own. If it was allowed to, Nin would fire my ass."

Frida stayed silent, listening to their footfalls echoing along the empty halls. The air was a touch too warm, and Frida noticed beads of sweat on her father's brow. Her stomach twisted. Maybe she should have let someone else go to the conference. She could have stayed home, even if it meant never meeting the stars or the moon. But, could she accept a life where she didn't seize opportunities? She didn't want to keep looking at the dome and wondering what was really out there, or run for shelters when an airlock blew. Humanity had poisoned this world, but with the galaxy being a touch more occupied than previously thought, there was nowhere else for the population of these worlds to go. They just made more domes, dug deeper levels and dreamed of having enough money to leave. *Can I really get off this rock?* Frida thought, as she realized that she'd never felt the warmth of sun on her skin or breathed the salty air on the seashore. The shallow muckpits of Nox hardly qualified as seas, but you couldn't breathe there regardless. Needless to say, now that she was on the ship, she would find herself adapting more easily to her imminent adventure.

"How long have you been working on this ship, Juke?" Zeke asked. His eyes darted around, taking in every sight and piece of information. Ever the engineer, he was seeing how things really worked in situ.

"About eleven years. Bounced around a bit, but Nin treats us good enough and the routes are safe. What else does a person need?" Juke replied, but her voice had a flatness that contrasted with her usual jovial tone. Frida wondered which voice reflected the lie.

"Have you been to Elym-One?" he asked.

"Oh yeah. Gorgeous place. Bright sun, perfect weather, everything is clean. They sure learned after the Nox disaster ..." She cut off quickly. "No offense, of course."

"I remember the times before the domes. I was very small. Feels like another person's memories now," Zeke said. "Times best left unremembered, perhaps."

"You never said you were there, Dad," Frida said.

"I try not to think of those days," he said. "Those memories make living in that world unbearable. They are as poisonous as the air."

"Why?"

Juke butted in. "Could you live a life without beauty once you'd lived in paradise?"

Frida considered that. The only beauty that wasn't a surgically augmented human was in her equations. "I suppose my work is beautiful to me."

"I hope that is never taken from you, Frida," her father said. "Mathematics is a source of objective truth that never grows old, never fades, never dies. It is perfect, in its own way."

Frida nodded. He understood her, at least.

"Mathematics?" Juke asked. "You should join us for liftoff, I can show you my course calculations."

Frida clasped her hands behind her back. "I'd like that," she replied in a small voice.

They turned another corner, finally coming to a large metal door, made of darker metal than the surrounding hallway. The number 819 was on an enameled plate, its white text gleaming in the artificial light. Frida tried to find meaning in the number, but none of her extensive studies had a relevant explanation. It simply was. The one feature of life, she found, was that coincidence did not exist. The numbers were probably meaningless. *As meaningless as humanity?* she wondered. She fought against the nihilistic thought, reminding herself that she was leaving Nox, if only for a while.

Juke hit a green button at elbow-height, and the door slid open, revealing a grim but efficient interior. The wall directly across from the door was one large window. Perfect for stargazing, but now all it revealed was the omnipresent fog of Nox-Gamma's toxic atmosphere. Frida looked down at the floor, the reminder of her world's true appearance robbing her of the triumph of being allowed off world. To the left was a set of bunk beds with simple gray blankets and supports. To the right were a pair of dressers made of plastic, and the door to a small lavatory. "You two are lucky, you get a private washroom. The discount travelers get to share one. Gotta be fun waiting behind ten others when you really have to go, eh?"

Zeke chuckled. "I've done worse, back when the domes went up. Probably not a story to share at the moment. Kinda gross."

"Come on Dad," Frida said as she walked into the room. "See ya on the bridge Juke."

"Got it, later math-girl." Juke left, the door sliding closed behind her noiselessly.

"She was cute," Zeke said. He had an eye for the ladies. As much as Frida did, even.

"Dad!" Her tastes weren't his business, but fathers would be fathers, she guessed. "You're never this way with my boyfriends!"

"What, a guy can dream. So can you, if you look up from your tablet once in a while. Boys are boring, face it."

Frida pulled her luggage over to the dresser, and pulled open a drawer. "You wouldn't know, Dad. Say, I've never even left Dome-12 before. Now look at me. Unpacking, flying away to damn Elym-One and giving talks about stuff nobody cares about. I'm living every girl's dream."

"That's how to look at it. Enjoy the trip. Maybe we can even figure out how to move there, right? It's gotta be better than this dead world, with canned air and a glow globe for a sky." Zeke stroked the small goatee that infested his chin with gray hair.

"I wouldn't know."

Zeke rubbed his hands together. "Just wait for liftoff. When we clear the barrier, you'll see. You'll never experience the universe in the same way again after this trip."

"Let's go. I'm ready for this," she said, but her stomach was turning in knots. Juke, flight, space. What kind of adventure would it be? Additionally, could this trip off-world be the start of a better life?

Chapter 2

The double metal doors slid open and the intense brightness of the bridge lights caused Frida to blink to clear the dancing spots that had formed. Captain Nin was sitting front and center, leaning on the arms of her high-backed chair and immersed in her tablet. Juke sat to the side, facing the view screen, her green balls resting on the console in front of her in a small holder. A few other crew were settled at their stations, plucking away at buttons and ignoring their approach. A few others in civilian clothes milled around, some sat along a bench at the rear of the bridge, flanking an imposing set of sliding doors. Frida watched Zeke for a moment before stepping in. She observed him scan the crowd and grimace, but she couldn't discern the object of his ire.

Nin turned to face the new arrivals. "Finally made it? Make yourself comfortable, but don't bother my people or get in the way. If you do, you get to meet Kazik while he's on duty, and trust me, you don't want that." She nodded to a large long-haired man in red coveralls standing in the corner. His arms were folded and somehow he was managing to give the evil eye to everyone in the room, simultaneously. The small hairs on the back of Frida's neck rose as his eyes fixed on her. She swallowed and looked to her dad, who was successfully ignoring Kazik. Must be something to do with age, being able to not react to intimidation. Frida turned back to Nin, then looked around the bridge. Frida grabbed Zeke by the arm and led him to a set of chairs by the sliding doors.

"Don't do anything to embarrass me, Dad," she whispered.

"Who, me?" he replied. "Never."

Frida leaned back and looked out the view screen, her fingers digging into the arms of the chair. The image was one of pure wonder for her, colossal ships lifting off and landing with seemingly no effort, and the air outside was clear! If the city's dome covered this section of the space port, there was no indication of it on the screen. Ships of all makes and colors came and went, but silently, as the ship must be very well insulated to survive the rigors of space travel. Frida's eyes traced what looked like a great metal bird, swooping in from the heavens to land in a precise spot. Then, a crew in protective suits ran out, connecting the tethers and airlocks. They worked in lockstep, as one, and Frida could sense an almost mathematical pattern to what they did. Everything was a design on Nox, after all. Breaking protocol would get you injured—or worse. Air was life.

Nin chuckled from behind her. "Just wait until we clear the dome, Frida. You've seen nothing like space. The sims might look like it, but they aren't anything like flying through the real deal, engines humming around you. Nothing like it. Come on Juke, get this party started already."

"You got it, boss," Juke replied, turning her attention to her console. She placed a visor over her face, making a hell-red glow on her eyes. "You wanna come watch, Frida? You might like some of these equations. Very elegant." She motioned her over, smiling.

Frida gingerly got out of her seat after Nin nodded her ascent, and walked over to Juke, heart beating fast. The other woman's presence was comforting, and Frida liked knowing what was going on. She'd flown in simulations a few times, but this was going to real space, not historical simulations of what Nox used to look like. Big difference. Juke's fingers flew over the controls. It all made sense. Frida suspected that there were things she couldn't see, because she wasn't wearing a visor, but coordinates and thrusts she could read, and she studied the setup and controls of the ship. It was similar to the sims, but this was real. And much cooler. As though she'd read her mind, Juke said, "The visor lets me transmit my thoughts to the Dome's space port control, so my voice doesn't distract the others. If I'm needed, Aesop will ping me. Don't worry, it's just for on-planet use. I don't usually wear red shades."

A few deft keystrokes proceeded, and Juke seemed to go into a brief trance before announcing, "Dome-12 space control has cleared us for take off." A few voices muttered from behind.

Nin flipped a switch on a small console to the left of her chair, and Juke responded by pressing a button on the top right of her console. A high-pitched whine filled the air for a moment, then it was gone and a small light on Juke's console turned red. Party time, as Nin had said.

Frida jolted upwards in her seat as the ship came alive. The air was charged with energy and the surfaces hummed with great potential for adventure—and danger. The lights in the bridge dimmed, making the controls more prominent and Juke's red visor glared against the walls nearest to her. The view screen tracked their movement, first horizontally along the ground, away from the safety of the Dome and the umbilical cords of the airlocks and ports, and towards the center, where only a force field protected them from the dangers of Nox's atmosphere and the dreaded vacuum of space itself. Then, they pitched upwards, the shimmering green of the force field dancing over the twisted miasma of yellow and brown that was what was left of Nox's atmosphere. Frieda held her breath, refusing to blink, fused in place. She needed to be ready for when they hit the field. When they left what had been her home for all twenty seven years of her life.

In an instant, the green static vanished, leaving only the nightmarish swirl of noxious colors dancing before her. Every part of her that was human knew it was wrong. The sky shouldn't look like that. That was as fundamental as the Pythagorean Theorem. The sky was not supposed to be toxic. The sky was supposed to be a blanket, soft and kind. A force of creation and freedom, rather than one of smothering cruelty.

Gasps echoed behind her. The clouds were gone, leaving a pristine and exquisite black that enveloped all. It was the cleanest thing Frida had ever seen. The stars poked through, making patterns only known to the heavens themselves. They were beautiful. And, for the first time, she knew they were real. A hand went to her mouth, and her mind was blank. All trepidation melted away, replaced by the starry night. This was right. This was human. Had her ancestors marveled at the stars as she did now?

The red glow cast about the room turned off, and an arm circled her shoulders. "How about that for the first time?" Juke asked.

"That was incredible, I never thought ..."

"Yeah, I know. Go back to your dad, we can chat when I'm off. I'll be in the bar, say 'hi' to Glizzy for me."

Frida stood up, and walked back to Zeke. He beamed at her, his near-black eyes reflecting the lights from around them. "How was that?"

"Yeah ..." Frida started, her eyes trailing to Juke.

Nin stood over Juke's shoulder, pointing at her tablet. Nin was giving orders. "Take the shortcut through the Molorus sector. We'll get there ten days faster. Shore leave on Elym-One sounds good for all of us."

Juke replied, "Molorus? You sure boss?"

Nin began to say something, but Kazik appeared, ordering everyone off the bridge. Frida took one last look behind her, watching Nin and Juke discuss their route. What was in the Molorus sector, and why did Juke seem hesitant? Frida made a mental note to research further, as her father guided her back towards their quarters.

"Let's do some stargazing before dinner. Don't want to meet all these people on an empty stomach," he said. "It's been so long since the accident, I'd almost forgotten ..."

"Yeah, Dad, I know. You gotta tell me one thing, though."

"What?"

"Did the stars always look like that?" she asked.

"You know, I don't really remember. I was just a kid, you see. Things seem warped when you're young. When you're as old as I am, you'll see the truth in that," he replied.

Frida shivered, the narrow walls of the ship crunching in on them, threatening to steal the air and smother them. Even the Dome wasn't this disorienting. Her father put his hand on the small of her back. "Dad?"

"You'll be okay. Just don't forget to breathe. You'll get used to it," he said.

"Says the retired engineer who spent his life digging in the underground," she shot back at him.

"It was a living. Had to raise your ass on my own, didn't I?" he replied.

He had her with that one.

Chapter 3

Frida stared out the window, transfixed by the streaks of blue and red light and smears of color. These were the stars and various nebulae and constructs of the heavens. It was so different, compared to the solemn blandness of the Dome and the death-sky of Nox. Her father lay on his bunk, eyes closed, his soft breathing overlaying the hum of the ship. Frida wasn't sure what to do. She held her tablet, but had been too absorbed by her initiation into the universe to look at the ship's layout, or research the Molorus sector. Nin and Juke knew what they were doing, so what did it matter? She was weary of the constant distress of life on Nox. It was time to let someone else do the worrying. She was going to enjoy the view, and maybe get to spend more time with Juke. Maybe she should look for this bar and Glizzy character?

She considered Juke. Frida had never met anyone like her. Frida was fascinated in a way that didn't come easily. She didn't understand. People weren't that interesting, most were similar to the point of tedium. But this was a new world, with new individuals. Perhaps it would be a positive experience to explore humans, just this once.

"Dad, I'm going to explore," she said. She had designs on finding the bar, and experiencing a side of life she'd never experienced. Yes, it was a cargo ship, but anything that accepted passengers would have a view, lighting, a bartender who wasn't cooking swill in some bathtubs and drinks that weren't called Gutdoom.

"Don't get lost," he replied.

She walked out the door, her soft-soled shoes pattering along the steel floor. She held her tablet in front of her, trying to find the recreation room. Some relaxation and mingling should pass the time. Ten days on this crate, if this shortcut was taken into account. It felt almost interminable. The halls didn't help—empty and devoid of life, she always had the feeling she was being watched. *It's the security cameras*, she told herself. Just cameras and the computer. These were normal, right?

She sighed and walked into the rec room. It was immense, the length of the deck. There were gray chairs and couches placed with glass tables along the windows. A modest bar sat to the right, colored bottles neatly lined up. One person stood behind it, polishing glasses and looking about the room with a keen eye. Spiked blue hair and ethereal glowing green eyes struck Frida— nobody on Nox would style themselves in such a way. Nobody had the money to, or the will. Living under the Dome was to live the bleakest of existences. Even the tight confines of the Destiny were vibrant in comparison. The rest of the room contained some passengers who milled about, some who were seated and some standing and talking with glasses in hand. Nobody seemed particularly interested in the view, or the high-energy electronic music that was thankfully played at a moderate volume. Frida admitted that the void was losing her interest, so she didn't blame them for not stargazing. Was it getting darker ahead, or was that simply the natural progression of space?

The bartender motioned her over with an easy gesture and bright smile. "First time on a ship? What can I get you? I'm Glizzy" they said, with a voice that wasn't identifiable as male or female.

"Is it that obvious?"

"It is when you act like you've never seen a bar before," they said, putting a bulbous round glass up on the glowing blue countertop.

"Maybe I haven't," Frida said with a chuckle. Establishments of this caliber were for the upper skyscrapers in the Dome, and here she was, in a bar on a cargo ship. Suddenly, she realized she didn't want to go back to Nox.

"I know what you need," they said, turning to grab a square bottle filled with a twinkling liquid with darkening layers of of green. "This one's called the Green Blitzen."

Frida blinked. "What's a blitzen?"

"Glitched if I know, it's green and people like it," they said as they performed what could only be described as alcoholic alchemy. A shake here, a dash of another alcohol there, and a little umbrella to top it off. Frida had never seen a real umbrella before. "Here you go, make yourself comfortable, don't gamble money you don't have and don't spill that on Pesky, or Nin will have your ass."

"Gotcha." Frida swanned off, looking at the people who were there to converse, or exist, or perhaps neither, depending on the alcohol content of whatever Glizzy dreamed up. She wondered if there would be dancing. She did love to watch the movements of those who had imbibed too much in the vids. It was a guilty pleasure.

Coming to an armchair by the window, she eased herself down before setting her tablet on the table. Taking a sniff of her drink, she tilted her head before daring to taste it. Her lips puckered at the tang, but the sweetness and fruity essence danced on her tongue, giving the feeling of small exploding rocks. *Not bad, Glizzy.*

She nursed her drink, careful not to take in too much at once. She'd only had alcohol a few times, when she'd had a good payday at work or won an award for her academic skills. Even then, it was always some kind of watery ale. Part of her wanted to taste and try everything, but her common sense knew that to be a very bad idea.

Setting the drink on the table, she picked up her tablet and reviewed their flight plan. It had been approved by the Galactic Council as the safest route between Elym-One and Nox-Gamma. But, there was the question of the proposed shortcut. She looked up the Molorus sector, and frowned. It wasn't near the front lines, but it also wasn't inhabited. Could there be pirates there? Whispers of dread pirates of human or other descent floated through society like a foul breeze. The Destiny was but an unarmed cargo ship, why would they go there?

"Hey kid," Zeke said, having a seat. He had a swirling red-blue drink in hand. "Hitting the bar already?"

"I'm twenty seven, Dad, not fifteen. This is way better than the bars back home. You know, dark, dead-step music, homemade and potentially spiked drinks. How could I resist?"

"Done drinking piss ale and bathtub swill, finally?" He sniffed at his drink before testing a small sip. He cocked his head for a moment, then took another sip.

"You could say that." She leaned back in her chair, looking up from her tablet. "Dad?"

"Yeah, punk?"

"Do we have to go back?"

Zeke let out a long sigh. "Leave it all behind and start anew? Your work, your friends? Our home and the rats who live in the walls?"

"I can move on. They'll be happy for me. The Dome ..." she said, trailing off for a moment.

"What about the Dome?"

"It's not real. Humans aren't made to live that way. You remember, don't you? You keep talking about it today."

"I remember." He hung his head, looking at the pad. "Tell you what, while you're doing your thing, I'll figure out how to get us in. But."

"But?"

"Lay off the alcohol. All this talk of unrealness can creep out the wrong kind of people. Most of them are just along for the ride, a bit too much thinking will ruin their buzz."

She pushed her almost empty glass away from her and cast her father a wicked smile. "Deal."

Chapter 4

"And that's how I managed to visit all twenty one allied planets in under a year," Juke said, before draining her amber Aljerion mead and putting down the fluted glass. The room murmured with activity, people flitting in and out. Drinks glowed, the music droned on and the lights were dimmed. A few sad fools even tried their luck at dancing, but in reality looked like they were trying to balance in the middle of an earthquake. Frida and Juke sat at a table, alone in the corner. Zeke had excused himself quickly, as though he understood his daughter's curiosity and fascination with the other woman. *Thanks, Dad.*

"But how did you get through the blockades? The front lines?" Frida asked, playing with her hair. To talk to someone who had been outside a Dome, and off-world at that, was incredible. Above and beyond that, Juke wasn't a stuffy academic dignitary. She had experienced a different kind of life.

"The Captain is a resourceful woman, she knows all the tricks." Juke winked.

"I'm sure you did your part, too," Frida replied.

Juke chuckled. "I just make the music to someone else's tune."

Frida pondered that for a moment. "In a way, we all do, as sound does not exist alone. Without you, there could be no art to it."

Juke sat back. "Do you like art?"

"I think so, not much art on Nox," Frida said. "I have a question, Juke."

"Shoot."

"What's in the Molorus sector?"

Juke arched an eyebrow. "How'd you hear about that?"

"On the bridge, remember? Before Kazik kicked us all out I heard you and Nin talking."

"Oh, it's nothing. Just a sector of space with nothing in it. No planets of use, few stars."

"So what's the big deal?"

Juke smiled. "Usually the boring things are the most forbidden. But, ten days off, paid, on the richest planet in the twenty-one colonies. Think of the possibilities," she said with a grin.

Frida saw her chance. "Got any plans?"

"Well, maybe a museum or two."

What. "Museum?"

"Yeah, why not? Don't you appreciate beautiful things? Culture? You studied, right?"

"Nothing about Nox is beautiful."

Juke nodded. "Yeah, been there enough times. Those damn Domes. But, beauty can be found anywhere. You just need to see it. That's beautiful."

"I see beauty in many ways, I learned how," Frida admitted.

"Like?"

"In my equations, I can see so many things. And, they're the same no matter where you are. They're intangible, but it's the closest thing I've ever had."

"Never was that good at math," Juke admitted. "I just have a knack for coordinates and good reflexes."

"But, you make your coordinates dance, and you can fly a ship!"

"Just don't ask me to prove a theorem and I'll let you go on believing that."

"Say, Juke?" Frida licked her lips, not sure how to ask what would come next.

"Yeah, Frida?" Juke looked at her.

"When we get to Elym, can I come with you to one of these museums?"

"Sure, I'd be glad to have you along." Juke smiled at her and stretched. "It will be nice to have company. Nobody here gives a shit about art," she said.

Frida could barely contain her excitement. "But how will I find you?"

"When we're in range I'll get you set up with galactic credentials. All travelers should have them. You going back to Nox?"

Frida shook her head. "I hope not. Smoke knows I've had enough of that place."

"Smoke?"

"Yeah, the air. What's left of the water. The color of the domes. It's all smoke. Smoke and ozone. That's all there is. All there ever will be." Frida's eyes stung. She couldn't go back and live with herself, knowing she could have left and had a real life. A life of vitality, safety and health.

Juke made a face. "Yuck. Understood."

"Dad and I are going to try to stay on Elym-One. We'll get jobs somewhere and start over. New lives," Frida spoke quickly, giving witness to her and her father's plans for the first time.

Juke nodded. "What do you expect to find on Elym, though?"

"I've never even felt the sun on my skin before," Frida replied. "I want the sun, a moon, wild animals that aren't rats and cats, plants growing everywhere. These things called birds that sing. Water that's clean and blue. A life away from the crime lords and riots. You don't know what Nox is really like. The entire planet is a disaster."

"Really?" Juke asked, as another mead was put in front of her.

"Yeah. Can't go out without a hazard suit on."

"Damn, I never considered that. I'm from Klinet, we have two suns. It's glorious to just lather up and bask in the heat. I suggest you visit it sometime, if you're into seeing real daylight. Just don't get burned."

Frida's brow knotted. Bask? Heat? Burned? The Dome was always the same temperature, the ambient light was always the same intensity, there was no wind. Before she could speak, the engines lurched, interrupting the constant hum of the ship for an instant. She braced herself against the table and looked around. The lights didn't dim, nor did the music go to static. The crowd's constant chatter quieted, before returning to its usual level. "What ... what was that?" she asked. Ships didn't just cut out, did they?

Juke shrugged. "That's just the engines making a course adjustment. I programmed it earlier today."

"But, why did we feel it? Shouldn't that be, you know, automatic?"

"The ship's slightly old. They may have put a few replacement parts on the back burner. We drop speed a bit sometimes, but we always pull through in the end. The engineer and I got this, don't you worry."

Frida let go of the table. "Okay." She offered a weak smile.

"You'll get your space legs, give it a day or two. I believe in you," Juke said. "Just breathe."

Frida put her hands in her lap, to hide their shaking. The sense of being watched had returned. It was a presence from all around, which even seemed to emanate from within her own body. Must be nerves, or the booze.

"You look like you could use a change of scenery. How about I walk you around the ship, show you the glorious sights of an obsolete cargo junker?" Juke winked.

Frida smiled. "Yes!"

Juke downed her mead and stood up. Her bare shoulders glistened in the light, her high wavy black ponytail danced. She extended a hand.

Frida took Juke's outstretched hand and stood up. The dubious qualities of alcohol spread to her head, and her cheeks heated. She allowed Juke to lead her out of the bar, and down an unfamiliar passageway. The space was dark, but there were strips of yellow lights along the top and bottom of the corridor. Juke's grip tightened around hers, its strength and softness mingling. Frida never wanted to let go. She couldn't believe she'd been concerned about this voyage, something about this adventure seemed so right, so predetermined. Frida doubted the concept of destiny, but it was fun to imagine the paths her other lives could have taken. Other partners, other schools, other jobs. Her mother surviving and living long enough to raise her into adulthood. Frida pushed that thought out of her mind, returning to the present. The present, where she was in the company of someone unique. Special, perhaps?

"So, tell me Frida, what do you think of the stars?" Juke asked. "I understand you'd never seen them before."

"They're very different from the pictures. Each seems to have its own place, its own soul."

Juke chuckled. "Right you are. Everywhere I've traveled is a sacred place, with its own special energy. Different biomes, cultures, languages. All beautiful in their own ways."

They turned another corner. "Even Nox? Earth?" Frida asked.

"Even destruction can have an art to it. The universe, like art, is an abstract concept."

Just like in the equations. "Some would disagree."

"I would encourage some to travel and read more," Juke said. They came around another corner, and a small door lay at the end. Juke pressed her palm against a scanner and the portal slid open, revealing a small recreation area. "The crew's private relaxation area, for those of us who want some quiet. You can't come in here alone but if you're with one of us it's fine." She motioned to a gray couch.

Frida took a seat on the well-worn sofa, the piece of furniture threatening to devour her. Juke sat next to her. "Now, I saw on the manifest you're somewhat of a scholar."

"I pretend to be," Frida would never stoop to the conceit of calling herself a scholar in any real sense of the word, but it was still nice to hear.

"Nonsense. Pretenders don't get off of Nox."

Frida swallowed and nodded. "Juke?"

"Yeah?"

"Can you tell me about the galaxy?"

Juke squeezed her hand. "Nothing would please me more."

Chapter 5

Frida's head spun as they walked back to her quarters. It was late, or perhaps early, on a ship it was impossible to tell without a chronometer. Her voice was hoarse, having spent the evening discussing the universe in ways she'd never thought possible. There were few whose company she could seek out and feel at home and understood in. Her father was one, along with a rare friend or two who flitted in and out of her existence. Juke was something else altogether. Frida forced down the growing infatuation, using the cold logic that they both had very different paths in life. It could not happen. But, what if it could?

A squeak shook her from her semi-drunken reverie, and she started. Her eyes scanned the hallway. The noise happened again. Was it another engine glitch? A loose panel? Depressurization? Her heart beat faster and she pulled back against Juke's grasp.

"That's just Dumbass, silly. Get over here, cat" Juke called.

Another squeak came, this time sounding more like a cat. There were cats on Nox, skulking in the street corners eating vermin and begging for scraps. A lithe tabby rounded the corner, tail held high as it strutted towards them. Juke knelt down, stretching out her free hand. "Come on, Dumbass, say hello."

The cat rubbed itself against Juke's outstretched hand, its stripes playing in the dim light. An audible purr could be heard, and the cat's big green eyes contemplated Frida as it tilted its head. Probably knows I'm different, she thought. She reached out, patting the creature's soft fur. It arched its back towards her touch. The cats on Nox weren't this soft, and seldom looked this healthy. The rats were contaminated meat, and anything in the so-called natural food chain showed the planet's taint. "Hi, Dumbass," she said.

The cat rolled over, exposing its belly. Frida reached for it, before being cautioned off. "It's a trap," Juke said.

"What?"

"He does that so he has an excuse to claw you. Let's get you back to your dad. Can't have him thinking you've been consorting with the crew all night long, can we?" Juke winked. Giving Dumbass a final pat, Frida rose to her feet. Juke pulled her closer, and wrapped an arm around her shoulders. Frida wondered if she looked that unstable.

"Is it much farther?"

"You're just around the corner. Meet again tomorrow after my shift?"

"I'd like that very much," Frida said, beaming.

Juke faced her, a small smile on her face. "Good night, then, but first ...." She let go of Frida's hand, and cupped her face. Juke leaned in, their lips pressing together for an instant before the contact melted away into the cosmic night.

Frida watched Juke walk down the hall, then pressed her hand to her lips. They still hummed with the touch, her nose filled with the citrus tones of Juke's choice of shampoo. She turned and rushed to her quarters, hoping her father was already asleep. She didn't want to endure a round of taunting. Teasing for what? She was only human, after all.

***

Frida sat in the bar with her father, this time nursing a non-alcoholic drink called orange juice. An Earth delicacy, she had been told. It was doing wonders for the headache, preceded by a special liquid treatment that tasted like fire courtesy of Glizzy. Apparently, it was the cure for what ailed her. Frida wasn't so sure, but she'd tolerate anything that could make the pain go away. The room was filled with electronic music, hopeless dancers, and the quarrels of drunken conversation, much like the previous night. She and her father sat in armchairs around the same glass table in the corner, with room for another. They were both reading. The long voyage made conversation a surplus resource and they seemed to have run out of things to talk about. Aside from a few more stalls, nothing had happened. Not for them. The passengers could spend their leisure hours at Glizzy's mercy, getting plastered and swaying like idiots. Frida wondered if that was a happier existence than hers. Mindlessness was a freedom all in itself.

"Is this seat taken?" A male voice interrupted her thoughts, his words slurred and the smell of alcohol hung like a miasma around him.

Frida glanced up. The man of about a century old had gray hair and a long nose. He was wearing a blue suit that could only have come from the sweatshops of lower Nox. His face had the deathly pallor of one who never saw the sun, and his eyes clawed at her. She suppressed a shudder. "We're waiting for someone, sorry," she said.

"You sure?" he asked, slithering into the seat. "I think you'd like me once you got to know me."

"Leave my daughter alone," Zeke said, placing his tablet on the table. His voice was a low growl. "She said no and you will respect that."

"Yeah, she's that little tramp running around with the skank working the helm. Some daughter. You ought to be ashamed, my old friend."

Frida stood up. "Get out."

"Or what? Don't you know who I am? I'm Lus Mikled, and I own half of lower-Dome 12. I can buy both your asses, can't I, Zeke?"

"Go to Hell, Lus, before I show you what I really think of your business acumen," Zeke said.

Frida had enough. Her hands shook and her cheeks heated. All she could feel was disgust for this creature posing as a man. One that embodied all that was wrong with the teeming humanity trapped on Nox. "Own this," she said, as she grabbed the glass of orange juice and splashed it in his face.

He recoiled, knocking the chair over. "You bitch!" he howled, as he skulked off, wiping his face on his sleeve.

Frida stood, frozen in place, the eyes of the entire room on her. Then she sank into her chair, clasping her hands in her lap.

Her father laughed. "Nice job, kid. Lus has been asking for that for ages. Have you been watching the news?"

Frida shook her head. "It sounds like you had a score to settle with him."

Zeke paused for a moment. "A story for another time, I'm afraid."

Glizzy appeared by their table's side, as if by magic. "Normally, I don't encourage baptism by orange juice. But, you did just get that moron out of my bar for a bit." They put down a mug of a steaming brown liquid. "Try an apple cider. Calms the nerves. On the house."

"Thanks, Glizzy," Frida offered a weak smile.

"Just remember, keep it off the carpet next time you teach some pervert humility."

The crowd turned back, the show clearly being over. The hum of conversation returned. After Glizzy was back behind their bar, Frida spoke, "Did he mean what he said?"

"Lus, you mean?"

"Yes."

"You don't get that much influence down below through being nice." Zeke looked down at his hands. "Trust me."

"Oh."

Zeke sighed. "All the more reason to not go back. He can do nothing to us off-world. There, he's just an old guy in an ugly suit."

Frida opened her mouth, but was interrupted by a sudden creaking of metal. It rippled through the room, not like percussion, but a vibration. It reminded her of passing through the force field on the way onto the ship, but evidently metal didn't appreciate transitions. "What was that?"

Zeke looked around. The crowd milled about, and the dancers had stopped moving. Everyone stood, their mouths agape. "I don't think that was a brief engine glitch."

"No, no that wasn't." Frida suspected that this voyage was about to become much more interesting than a cute helms woman and angry mobster. If there was something wrong with the ship, what was there she could do? She was a mathematician, not an engineer or technician. Frida sipped her apple cider and stared out the window. There was no going back. Not to Nox, and not off this ship.

Chapter 6

"What was that rumbling earlier?" Frida asked, as she walked hand in hand with Juke through the ship's halls. They'd excused themselves and had spent the hours wandering through the ship, sometimes meeting others, and once having the pleasure of encountering Pesky outside the crew's recreation room. All was quiet, only the pervasive hum of the engine and their synchronized footsteps could be heard.

There were no signs of problems, no indications that anything untoward had happened. No announcement from Nin, and Glizzy offered a round of free ales to help loosen up the crowd and get the dance party back underway. Juke thankfully arrived soon after, as Frida wasn't keen on being in a crowd when something anomalous was evident. And drunken morons could be dangerous in large groups, Zeke had warned her.

"What rumbling?" Juke asked.

"Kind of like a vibration, the entire hull of the ship seemed to shake. On Nox, it could mean a blown airlock, or a crack in the superstructure, or..."

Juke cut her off. "Was this just a few hours ago?"

"Yeah, like during Glizzy's happy eternity party."

"Don't worry about that. We were just passing into a different phase of warp speed inside a solar system. This particular system can be turbulent so the ship needed to adjust quickly. Nothing I can't handle! Just drink more, then you won't notice so much."

"The effect is that pronounced? Doesn't that mean the hull is weak or something?"

"Can be, but the hull is fine, Nin sees to that. The shields disperse the irregularities from the turbulence." Juke squeezed Frida's hand. "Everything is fine, I promise."

"Okay, I believe you," Frida said. The knot in her stomach loosened slightly, but the shakiness persisted.

"Hey, I have an idea, want to see the cargo bays?"

"Sure, why not." Could it really be that interesting? However, Frida would agree to just about anything Juke suggested at this point, so she wasn't going to argue.

Juke led her to a large double door on the lowest deck of the ship. Frida tried not to think that she was less than a meter from the vacuum of space. She shuddered. Upon Juke activating the hand print lock, the door slid open. A black void lay beyond the threshold, threatening to swallow them whole. Juke stepped through, and instantly the lights snapped to life. Tall rows of bins, each brightly colored like children's building blocks, sat parallel to each other. The ceiling was high, taking up at least two decks and the solid steel was punctuated by lazy circular fans. The rows of containers continued endlessly—the bay seemed to stretch the entire length of the ship.

"It's not much of a park, but I figured it would be better than endlessly wandering the halls," Juke said.

Frida smiled. "It's perfect."

They walked down the right side, picking a row at random. Juke slid her hand from the small of Frida's back to her shoulders, pulling her close. The touch was electrifying, sending prickles down her spine and even into her toes. Frida smiled as her muscles loosened and her heart raced. Why was it so different this time? Was it the newness of the situation she found herself in, or someone who was a complete unknown quantity to her? Either way, it was intoxicating. Thoughts broke down, and were replaced by a base awareness of Juke explaining the finer points of navigating through an asteroid belt.

Juke stopped, and pulled Frida in close, wrapping her arms around Frida in a tight embrace. Frida's arms returned the gesture as though they had done this thousands of times, a lover's embrace in the heart of a cargo bay. Juke's hard muscles flexed as she leaned in, pressing her lips against Frida's forehead. The heat spread, and Frida lifted her face so her lips met Juke's.

A crash interrupted their embrace, followed by the sound of creaking metal. Frida jumped, and Juke pulled back, a frown etched on her face. "That's not supposed to happen," she said.

"Maybe it just fell?"

"No, these bays are inertially dampened, and isolated from the rest of the ship. Nothing gets in, nothing gets out without one of us being here. I gotta report this," Juke said, releasing her hold on Frida, her hands caressing Frida's shoulders before she reached in her pocket. It was a hand-held phone. "Alert Captain," she said, and the screen came to life.

Captain Nin's voice groaned over the speaker. "Aren't you off duty?"

"Yes, but there may be an issue with inertial isolation in cargo bay one."

"I'll order some diagnostics. Leave the investigation to engineering."

"Got it."

The screen went blank and Juke replaced her phone in her pocket. "Busted," she said with a sigh.

"Right when it was starting to get good," Frida said. Just her luck.

"Let's get out of here and I'll walk you home. The captain is probably gonna hand my ass to me in a few," Juke said.

"Why? I thought you were allowed in here."

"Yes, the girl who flies the ship has a date in the cargo bay in the off hours. You know the security video of that one is going to hit everyone's phones by the time my shift starts." Juke shook her head. "Totally don't need that kind of attention in my life."

Frida's cheeks reddened. "Crap. You gonna get into trouble?"

"Nah. I don't usually get involved with passengers, and my colleagues often pry into things that aren't their business."

"I see."

Juke pulled out her phone again. "You got one of these, right?"

Frida retrieved a small, basic model that was popular on Nox from her pocket and waved it in the air. "Like this?"

"Give me your contact, I'll send you the video," Juke giggled.

Frida tapped her phone against Juke's, and it pinged softly to signify that the exchange had been made. "Typically, you exchange numbers before the first kiss you know," she said.

"Must have forgot that one. Been on this damn ship too long."

They stepped back into the hallway and moved towards the elevator. "Ever thought of doing something else?" Frida asked.

"Sometimes. Maybe teach once my reflexes are dull, or I want to settle down. Design ships. A girl can dream."

"I've found that dreams are often the only thing that can truly motivate us."

Juke simply nodded as they entered the elevator. The lift moved to deck eight with a speed Frida found surprising for a ship in this condition, and they stepped out.

"Juke?" she asked.

"Yeah?"

Frida licked her lips. She'd just said the words, and the realization hit her. She had dreams. New jobs, new planets. New people. It was time to act, and get what she wanted out of life. "How about we pick up where we left off?" she asked, forcing herself to speak the words.

Juke's eyes opened wide for an instant, then she grinned. "Nothing would make me happier. Let's go this way," she said, leading them back to the elevator. Frida's headache was all but forgotten. It was going to be a good night.

Chapter 7

Juke sat up in her bed, the void of space provided her small but familiar quarters with a familiar wallpaper. There was a desk that held a computer terminal and her phone. Some paper books sat on a high shelf. They were her secret indulgence, a throwback to a childhood spent in the library reading about faraway places. These books held in their pages pictures of the art of old Earth, before a war had destroyed the museum that had housed the artifacts. Even thinking of it made her quake with rage. So much was lost. All the better that she was on this ship, with her crew mates, far from the vulgarity of politics and war. She considered the night before. How could it work? Frida was an intellectual, a truly gifted person with a future. Juke was a nomad, whose only ties to the intellectual world were self-taught. She sighed. It was an indulgence that could hurt both of them. *Why am I so weak?* she admonished herself, but after the thought came another: *Because she sees you, and I see her.*

She padded across the room in her bare feet, the cold metal floor chilling her toes. She picked up the phone and turned it on. A flood of messages popped into existence. Only one mattered. Frida. Her post was precise and perfect, just like her.

[*Frida Juniper*]: Had a great time last night. See you after work. Don't forget the video!!!!

Chucking, Juke checked the rest of the messages. There, at the top, was the soon-to-be-infamous video. *Laugh your asses off, I had a better night than you jerks*, she wanted to write, but she chose to remain professional and say nothing. They could leave the rest to their sick imaginations. She saved a copy of the flick and forwarded it to Frida. *Something to remember me by*, she thought. The room had an aura to it. Juke brushed it off as being the memory of a good night, mixed in with the touch of embarrassment at their exposure. She looked around before shaking her head. Frida had left in the dead of the night. She was alone, ready for yet another day at the helm, running endless tests and simulations.

While she was flipping through the rest of the messages and preparing to go for breakfast, there was a low rumble in her quarters. A memento from a long-forgotten adventure fell from the shelf, smashing into thousands of porcelain pieces. The hairs rose on her arms, and she stepped away from the mass of sharp shards.

A wave of air hammered into her, forcing her back against the wall. The center of the shelf was lifted up, crushed against the ceiling with a crunch of black plastic and the thud of books hitting the floor. More trinkets smashed, and the shelf hung from its fasteners, swinging in an unseen wind. The presence faded, nothing left in its wake.

"What in the realms was that?" she said aloud. Was it a containment failure? An artificial gravity error?

Juke knew better than to stay at the scene of the incident, especially not so close to a window. She donned a pair of green work coveralls and slipped on her shoes, and locked the door behind her. Pulling out her phone, she dialed engineering. "Hey eng."

"You again? What did you break this time? And when's the next video?" Branx's voice squeaked through.

Juke gritted her teeth. "Send a crew to my quarters. Weird anomaly tore up my room, not sure if it's grav or inertial." Competent as Branx seemed, he sure knew how to get under her skin. Must be his Terran upbringing.

"Oh, more fun last night?"

"Most like a replacement for my morning coffee. Which you will be, if you don't get to it," she said, her voice harsh. She had to get to the bridge.

"Fine, you're no fun."

Juke hung up on the jerk and double-timed it to the elevator. She entered deck ten on the control panel and waited, leaning against the wall with her eyes upturned. What a day this was going to be.

The doors opened, and she squared her shoulders and walked to her station. Her cheeks heated as she sat down, choosing to ignore everyone there. It would all blow over in a day or two. She logged in, ordering alerts with regards to repairs to her quarters. Frowning, she decided to also request information on the cargo bay. Why not? She was allowed to be curious. Not like anyone would notice the request, as long as the cargo was intact nobody cared. She idly wondered why both incidents had happened around her. Could it be a coincidence?

Her eyes widened. Frida.

Juke pulled out her phone, fingers flying as she fired off a message:

[*Juke*]: You okay?

It took only a moment, but she received a reply.

[*Frida*]: Doing great! We on for tonight?

Juke slumped back in her chair and breathed a heavy sigh. Frida was okay.

[*Juke*]: You bet! Drinks are on me.

45

Juke went back to work, planning their next date in the back of her mind. The only thought she had of the incident in her quarters was hoping her books weren't damaged.

Chapter 8

Frida stood by the crew lounge, her palms sweaty and clamped behind her back. Pesky wove between her legs, mewing and peering up at her with wide green eyes. Frida met the feline's gaze, only to have the cat coyly break contact and continue the cycle again. Why had Juke asked to meet her here on her lunch break? Frida's stomach sank as her mind raced through possibilities, all the worst-case scenarios. Had she done something wrong? She hung her head. It was typical—it seemed she was fated to be alone. Other than Dad. He was the one constant in her life.

"Frida!" Juke's voice called out, and Frida found herself wrapped in strong arms, and smooth skin nuzzling her forehead.

Frida held Juke tight. "Is everything okay?" she asked.

Juke took her hand and opened the lounge. "We need to talk about that," she said, her face unreadable.

Frida followed Juke in, and they sat in their usual sofa. Frida tried to disappear into her corner, wrapping her arms around herself. *Here it comes*, she thought.

Juke turned her head. "What's going on, Frida? Something bothering you?"

"There's something wrong, isn't there?" she asked.

Juke pulled one of Frida's cold hands to her chest. "Yes, but not with us."

Frida offered a small smile, her stomach settling. "So, what is it?"

Juke looked down before meeting Frida's eyes. "Something weird happened in my quarters this morning. I'm not sure what is going on."

"Okay, tell me about it."

"So, first I felt this weird wind. There's no wind in there, right? Then my wall shelf was hammered against the ceiling."

"What?"

"That's not all. Engineering found nothing. They probably didn't look that hard, but there were no malfunctions or anything of the sort in there."

"But, things don't fall up? I'm no physicist, but I know that much," Frida said.

"So I thought. But, here's the other thing. They found nothing in the cargo bay, either."

Frida stayed silent. It was unfathomable, how could such things be overlooked?

"Don't worry, I'm going to follow it up with the Captain. But ... be careful."

Frida nodded. "I will. How long until we get to Elym?"

"About eight days. Hopefully we'll get some repairs and I can forget all about this," Juke said, hesitating as she ended the sentence. Frida wondered if the incidents had destroyed Juke's illusions of security.

"You can show me some museums," Frida offered, changing the subject.

"Absolutely."

***

Frida and Zeke walked towards the bar, her father tossing the occasional jab about her taste in humans and asking if she preferred ship life to a quiet desk in the corner. Frida laughed as they entered the bar, the music subdued and the ceiling a shimmering cobalt. Glizzy stood behind their bar with their back turned, arranging and rearranging the bottles in a pattern only known to them. Frida couldn't decide. Were they organized by color, by amount filled, by type? So many possibilities. She pointed to her father "Let's go see the bar up close," she said.

Even being nearer, she was no closer to solving the problem of the bottle patterns. Similar liquids and bottles were grouped together, but she had no idea what they were. "Hey Glizzy," she called out, leaning her forearms on the glowing blue surface.

They turned, nodding. "What can I get you?"

"How do you order your bottles?" she asked. Zeke laughed. *Jackass*.

"The bottles are ordered however they want to be. I just listen."

Frida, in spite of all her education, could not make any sense of that statement. "That makes no sense. A bottle doesn't talk."

"It doesn't have to. Much like the universe, it just is. I just travel, obey its laws and try to make people smile." They grinned, showing off two rows of straight, gleaming teeth.

Frida giggled. "Well, when you put it that way, it makes perfect sense."

"I could tell you were a woman of logic. How about a drink?"

Zeke leaned in. "Teach her about rum this time."

"Rum? You got it! Do me a favor and turn around," Glizzy said.

"Why?" she asked.

"Do you want a drink or not?"

Frida rolled her eyes and turned, instead watching the drunks sway with the music. Tinkles and the sound of swishing liquid were going on behind her, but she didn't want to annoy Glizzy and peek. Her father leaned over and whispered, "You know, I have no idea what rum is," to her.

"Okay, check this monster out. No throwing it in anyone's face, I worked too hard on it." Frida turned, and Glizzy was grinning, producing two tall, curved glasses of brown bubbly liquid. "Its name is lost to time, but where branding forgets flavor always prevails. I found it in an old book when we stopped in on Earth a few years back."

Taking the beverage, Frida held out her phone to Glizzy's glowing payment processor. "Thanks, Glizzy."

"Don't look now, but your favorite person is coming to play."

Frida grinned. Juke wasn't due off for another hour. They were planning on having drinks and idling away the evening discussing the universe, their lives, and even just nothing at all.

She turned, and immediately recoiled. It wasn't Juke. It was Lus, the slimelord of Nox, a lecherous grin plastered across his face. *Oh no*, she thought. This couldn't be happening. Even having his eyes roving over her body made her want to retch. While she did like men on occasion, evil, greasy, and presumptuous weren't what she was into at all. Bile rose in her throat. She turned her back to him, pretending to find bottles of white alcohol on the wall fascinating.

Lus slithered in beside her. "Black coffee. Now."

While Glizzy worked their magic, Lus turned to her. "I see someone has been busy around the ship. Does daddy know what his little girl has been up to, I wonder?"

"My *little* girl is an adult, and can do what she wants. In fact, I encourage her to ruin that cheap suit of yours."

Lus chuckled. "This suit is worth more than this ship. So, Mr. Juniper, tell me, do you want a home to go back to? A good job perhaps?"

"I don't want to hear it. After what you've done, I'd rather starve in the muck."

Frida piped up. "I don't care what you want."

"You embarrassed me. I didn't appreciate that. I am a gentleman, and I insist on reparations. One evening of pleasant conversation with your brilliant daughter, and I'll forgive and forget." Lus looked Frida up and down. Her grip around the glass hardened, and she ground her teeth. That smoke-rat!

"You'd better walk away, now." Zeke stepped between Frida and the lecherous Lus, breaking the leering gaze he was casting on her chest.

Lus pushed him aside. "Think of your future. Your little girl is good enough for a cargo barge crew woman, but not for me?"

Frida set her glass down, balling her hands into fists. That bastard was not going to threaten her father, the man who'd given everything for her after her mother died. "She's better than you'll ever be," she said, forcing her voice to remain steady. She wanted to scream, to jump the bar and come back wielding two bottles of rum for some retribution. Her intellect restrained her instinct. A fight may be unavoidable, but she wasn't going to chance her future for this creature.

Glizzy appeared and set a coffee on the bar. "If you all continue, I'm going to have to ask you all to take this party somewhere else. Like security." They meant it, knotted brow and power pose showing Glizzy had been through this countless times before, and they meant business.

Lus held up his hands. "I would not think of causing trouble in your esteemed establishment, Glizzy. You both know where to find me when you decide to be sensible." He stalked off towards the seating.

Frida glared after him. She'd begun to shake, her breath hard in her ears. Zeke pulled her in for a tight hug. "He can't do anything to us, my light. We're going to Elym and he's going to spend his trip lonely. You hear me?"

Glizzy puckered their lips. "Always that one. Always him. Nin should ban him, I hate making his coffee."

"You know him, too?" Zeke asked. Frida was too paralyzed to talk. She wanted to vanish.

"Frequent flyer. Too cheap to take more luxurious accommodations. Just ignore him." Glizzy shook their head, their hair reflecting the dancing lights above the bar. "He's not actually gonna do anything. All talk that one."

Frida let out a slow breath. "Thank you, Glizzy," she said.

"Sit up here with me, enjoy your drink."

Frida hauled her butt up on a high bar stool, and her father followed suit. She took a sip of her mystery drink, letting the bubbles roll over her tongue. The cloying sweetness of it was surprising, but enjoyable. She could get to like this rum thing. "Dad?"

"Yes?"

"Will you tell me about mom, again?"

Zeke smiled, but sorrow touched the corners of his lips. "Anything for you, sweetie."

Frida sipped her drink and tried to remember her mother's face. The more her father talked, the more the image coalesced into a smiling figure. She took comfort in it, and the facsimile in her mind's eye comforted her as only a mother could.

Chapter 9

Juke sat in the briefing room, in the far back corner of its long redwood table. Nin sat at the front in the captain's seat, her expected position of command and authority. The room was encased in sound-proof glass, with a red line drawn at the median height mark. There was a screen in the center of the wall, powered on but with nothing on display. Juke held her hands under the table. *Why am I even here?* she wondered. She was not usually invited to these kinds of meetings. The engineering lead, Branx, sat across from her, squirming in his chair. A couple of the other officers were in their usual spots, elbows on the table, or engrossed in their devices. Kazik from Security was conspicuously absent. Juke's stomach was a knot. Was she in trouble? Was it about the incident? Did they want a tour of her quarters? Better yet, a good-natured hazing for the cargo bay incident could be in store for her.

Nin stood and cleared her throat. Her gaze flicked from person to person. The engineer made a valiant effort to sit still, but, as always, he failed. Nin licked her lips. "What we discuss here today does not leave this room," she said, crossing her arms in front of her chest.

Juke sat up. Was this about her quarters? The cargo?

"We have a saboteur on board."

Suddenly, all eyes were at full attention. Backs straightened. Devices were placed on the table. There was a brief murmuring. "How can that be? We inventory everything. Nothing living can get through that field!" Altur, the barrel-chested bald medic said.

"Something did," Nin replied.

"What are we looking for?" Juke asked.

"That's the tricky part, and given that you were present for the first two issues, it's interesting that you ask."

Juke shut her mouth in record time. Then, something clicked. "There were more?"

Nin nodded. "Security reported a sudden gravity reversal in crew quarters, coming close to crushing the passenger in the middle of the night."

Juke covered her mouth with her hand, while the other gripped her leg. Only the feeling of the presence had warned her away from the epicenter of the blast. She had to tell them, even if it sounded insane. "I felt something in my quarters just before," Juke said. "Like something was watching me, even inside of my body."

"Interesting, though unverifiable. I'll have the passenger interviewed for a ghost sighting," Nin said.

Juke slumped in her chair. At least she said her piece.

The captain continued: "For the moment, security is doing a sweep of all living and cargo spaces. Anyone in the crew, or passengers with the skills to interfere with ships systems, are to be interviewed. For the rest of you, stay out of places you're not supposed to be. Understood?"

Juke felt Nin's gaze rest on her, before it moved on to the rest of the staff.

"Dismissed."

Juke waited for the others to file out and then trailed after. She sat at her console, and frowned. She looked back and forth, checking for unwanted attention. When she was certain that everyone was engrossed in their duties, she accessed the security report on the latest occurrence. Filing it with the first two, she skimmed the data. There had to be a pattern. Juke longed to tell Frida about this. Frida's sharp mind and penchant for patterns could analyze any problem. For now, Juke would be forced to rely on her own intuition and skills. The incidents in the passenger quarters and her own experiences were almost identical. A sudden change in gravity. Like something had tried to push an object against a surface with great force.

Nothing could have prepared her for what she saw next. She gasped, and quickly turned off the screen, giving the illusion that she was working on her duties.

The infractions were exactly seven hours apart. Why hadn't that been noticed, or announced? Was Branx losing what was left of his touch? A chill ran down her spine. Was he the saboteur?

Troubled, she returned to her work, taking care to clear her data from her files. If Branx were the suspect, he was capable of anything. Even worse, he could see everything.

***

Juke picked at her lunch in the small break room adjacent to the bridge. Flavorless, brown, and of indeterminate origin, she forced the cubes into her mouth. With something like strange force of nature on the loose, nobody was safe. She gazed out the window, watching the streaking stars pass by. The dark patches of the Molorus sector punctuated the scene. Juke considered requesting to resign on Elym-One, and start a new life. On one hand, it was crazy to uproot your life for someone you just met.

On the other, she'd spent eleven years on this dingy tub. Being almost pulverized in her own quarters, seemed reason enough to move on.

"Mind if I join you? Old friends ought to talk once in a while, don't you think?"

Juke repressed a shudder. She'd know Branx's squeaky voice anywhere. "Go for it," she said. He was still a colleague, and thus requiring a modicum of respect.

The chair across from her dragged along the floor. Branx's skinny ass sat down, a package full of brown cubes in one hand and a flask of water in the other. "I see things have been interesting for you these past few days."

Juke didn't make eye contact. "I suppose."

"It's not every day you get a new girl and your room explodes." His bag of food rustled, and he chuckled in a fashion that made Juke suck in a deep breath. "Or any girl at all, knowing you." *Pig.*

"Say what you mean, Branx," she growled.

"I'm not saying anything. Just admiring coincidence. I'm happy for you, really, I am."

Juke shook her head and met his gaze. "Admire all you like. Shouldn't you be running a diagnostic or something right now? You know, do your job like the rest of us?"

"Unlike some of us, I can delegate. Unlike you, I have authority here," he said with a smile.

So he can be elsewhere, she thought. "Lucky."

"Yes, yes. You know, artificial gravity is really quite the marvel. Without it, we couldn't function. Especially not that bar you like so much."

Juke took a bite of her food and pretended to enjoy it, using chewing to refrain from replying. She wasn't going to dignify that with an answer.

"Anyhow, I shall be off. It's time I do real work. You know what that is, right flight monkey?"

Juke pointedly ignored him, opting to look out the window. Any old view beat looking at him.

"Nice talk. Stay out of the cargo bays." Branx stalked out the door, leaving her alone.

What was all that about? she wondered. *Does he know what I saw?*

For the first time in eleven years, Juke wanted off this ship. Just over a week to go. Was this really the end of a chapter for her? Could she move beyond the role of flight monkey?

Chapter 10

Frida moved her knight, capturing her father's white bishop. Chess had always fascinated her, and chess in the bar added an entire other layer of strategy—picking a table where a drunken moron wouldn't bump into it while trying to dance was almost as much of a strategy as the game itself. When she and her dad were locked in intellectual combat, the troubles of the world melted away. The bad music, the flash of the strobe lights on the chess pieces, and the ever present crowd no longer mattered. Her existence was relegated to a simple sixty four square board, and matching the considerable intellect of her father. This was their third game, and she had won the first two. If she was lucky, she'd win the third and he'd owe her a drink. That was their arrangement. Frida wondered how chess had passed the test of time, while countless other games had faded into oblivion. Humanity defined itself by the games it played. Perhaps chess was the epitome of that—trying to outmaneuver your opponent, consider all contingencies and probabilities while offering appropriate sacrifices, leading to a devastating checkmate.

"Damn,"her father muttered, scratching his head. His eyes scanned the board, flitting from piece to piece, trying to concoct some strategy to save himself.

Frida leaned back and smiled, the warmth of her impending victory mixing with the burn of alcohol. She wondered if she was turning into a drunk. "Come on, Dad. Time is finite for us," she said.

"You and your math, making your mother proud."

"At least I had a mother," Frida said. It made the senselessness of the woman's death sting less. Frida knew she had been wanted, and loved.

"Indeed you did." His queen slid across the board. "Check."

Check? That hadn't been in her strategy. She moved her king back, to the only place it could go.

The rook swooped down, its finality shocking Frida. "Checkmate."

Frida stared at the board. She hadn't lost a match to her father in years. Her brow knit, and she took another sip of her drink.

"Be wary of becoming overconfident, Frida," her father said. "The universe is full of cunning people who can prey on that."

She nodded. "Like Lus."

"We're going somewhere new. We have to take care not to be naive. Lus could be small fry compared to what we find there. We'll be new. We'll be alone. We have to be safe, unlike your king here." He took the piece between his fingers before letting it drop on the board. It clattered and rotated until coming to rest on a pawn.

She pursed her lips as she examined the board, trying for the last time to see her error. "Dad?"

"Yes, punk?"

"You could have beaten me all along, all these years?" She locked eyes with him, studying the lines of his face.

"You bet, kid."

She half-smiled and looked out the window. Overconfident, indeed. "What really happened to mom?"

Zeke folded his hands in front of his face, suddenly looking very much his age. "She tried to be a hero."

"Someone was in trouble?" she asked, looking over the crowd. Her father had never revealed the full story, just that it was an accident on her way home from work.

"It was a gang fight. Some of Lus's guys, back when Lus was just a little prick, started a brawl." He paused, staring at the empty air above her head. "Some of her students were in the crossfire."

Frida's heart sank. "Tell me. I need to know the truth."

"One of the best. Anyhow, she rushed to save one of her students, who was bleeding out." He closed his eyes and rubbed them with the back of his hand. "I've watched the vids over and over again. Trying to make sense of it. Just trying to understand."

"Why didn't you tell me?" Her eyes grew scratchy and her nose began to run. She sniffled. "How could you not tell me?"

"I didn't want you to grow up under the specter of hate and fear, or seek out Lus in any way. I wanted you to blossom. To be as beautiful as she had been. My dearest Klyessa." He rubbed his eyes again and sighed, a halting rattle that could only come from a deep pain.

"Dad, I ..." she began, not able to find the words. "All this time I thought it was an accident on the tram."

"Close enough, you're old enough to know the full truth, now you have it. Think on it before you bring it up again, Frida. Now, listen," he said.

"Yes?"

"This Juke of yours. Be careful with her," he said, his voice hushed.

"What makes you say that?" Frida asked. Juke couldn't harm anyone, Frida doubted it was in her nature.

"Because ... I can't tell which of you needs saving. You both suffer from a similar condition, and while it drives you together, it can also destroy you both."

Frida sat, dumbfounded. What could be said? Was it true, or just the words of a man afraid to lose the only person left to him? She reached out and held his forearm. "I'll be careful, Dad."

"Just remember," he said, clearing his throat, "even the most innocuous distraction can be deadly."

"I will, father."

***

Frida and her father were critiquing the finer points of drunken stupor dancing, as they called it, when Juke appeared. Her face brightened somewhat, but her lips were pursed together and her eyes scanned the room before sitting down. She was wearing her orange coveralls, with her hair loose and running down her shoulders. She gave a dismissive glance to the revelers, as though she'd seen it a thousand times before, and walked straight to Zeke and Frida's table. "Hey guys," she said, pulling out a chair. She looked over her shoulders. "Anything interesting going on today?"

"Dad beat me at chess, does that count?" Frida replied, neglecting to mention the evening's earlier conversation, glancing around the room. It wasn't like Juke to be uncomfortable in the bar.

"No, no ... I mean weird or odd."

"The guy in the white suit puked all over Glizzy's bar stool. That was pretty funny," Zeke said. "But, not odd for a bar of this caliber, no offense to Glizzy."

"Just a normal day, then," Juke said, as she pulled out her phone and checked the time. "Damn," she muttered.

"What is it? What's bothering you, Juke?"

Juke opened her mouth to answer, but froze in place and rubbed her bare arms. A tingling covered Frida's body, playing over and inside her skin. Frida got the impression that she was being watched, by some presence so powerful that it was able to see the entire room at once. An impossible breeze passed through the bar then. Frida looked around for any evidence of equipment failure. Or perhaps it was some sick game Lus was playing with her mind? Bastard.

"What the hell?" Zeke exclaimed. He looked around and moved to stand up, but froze mid-rise when he saw what happened next.

The man in the white suit at the bar straightened, eyes bugging out of his head. He swayed as he fought to stay upright. The crowd was transfixed. Glizzy dove to the far end of the bar, holding their arms in front of their face in a defensive posture. The man's name—Prak—was shouted out by his friends, but too late.

Noiselessly, Prak was lifted from the ground. His body smashed head-first into the ceiling before he could react. He didn't struggle. He didn't scream. He didn't even look up. Blood exploded from his body. His shape transformed from human to gory mass of splintered bone and liberated organs. His remains splattered to the floor, lumps of offal jettisoned into the crowd, the bar and those around it soaked in his body fluids. Glizzy's perfect hair was tainted with blood, their face masked in gore.

Screams echoed through the room. The door flew open, and the crowd ran out leaving the drunks trampled beneath their sober counterparts.

"Shit, shit, shit!" Juke screamed. "Get out!"

Frida clambered to her feet, forcing down the bile that had risen in her throat. A familiar copper scent permeated the air, and she could taste the haze of blood on her tongue. She grabbed her father by the hand and pulled him to his feet. They jumped over the twitching bodies of the injured party goers, and sprinted out the door. Red footprints splattered down both sides of the hallway. Juke followed them closely, pulling out her phone. "Captain, another incident in the bar. Multiple medical emergencies!" When she put her phone away, she turned to Frida and Zeke. "I have to stay here and make sure nobody goes in. Get yourselves somewhere safe."

"We'll stay with you."

"Frida ..." her father said.

"No, I can't put you both at risk. Go to your quarters, I'll meet you there after this is taken care of." Juke was shaking, her breath hard and fast.

Frida opened her mouth to argue, but her father dragged her down the hall towards their quarters. The bloody footprints became less pronounced as they rounded the corner, out of Juke's hearing range. "Remember what I said about rescuers, kid."

Chapter 11

Juke watched Frida and her father clear the corner of the corridor. Tears stung her eyes. The noxious smell and taste of blood permeated the air. She clasped her hands behind her back, waiting for security, medics, and the captain. Someone. Anyone. She especially wondered if Branx would show up. This time, the anomaly had gone beyond breaking furniture and cargo. It had pinpointed a human, with near perfect precision. The scene played over and over again in her mind's eye, and her stomach threatened to empty itself on the floor. Glizzy stumbled out of the bar, muttering to themselves. They were soaked in gore. Juke wondered if this would convince them to close shop and abandon working in space. Once safe in the hallway, Glizzy wasted no time in vomiting all over Juke's boots, adding another profanity to the already defiled floor. Juke forced herself to look at the ceiling while she rubbed Glizzy's back, offering the best comfort she could. There was no way she could unsee the atrocity that had just occurred, and here was poor Glizzy bathed in it.

Booted footfalls echoed along the hallway from both directions. Two gigantic security guards in black armor wielding clubs charged towards her, followed by the medic. Frida pitied the short, rotund man. Him against a room straight out of hell. Nin marched down the hallway as the guards and medic went inside the bar. A chorus of profanity followed before the door closed, isolating Juke from the noise.

"What the hell happened, Juke?" Nin asked, hands on hips and eyes like slits as she looked over the mess on the floor. She pinched her lips shut and quickly looked to the ceiling.

"Another anomaly, just like in my quarters. But ..." Juke paused, not sure what to say next. "You probably don't want to go in there."

"No shit," the captain sighed. "I can't hide from this. I'm in charge."

Juke nodded and leaned against the wall as the captain hunched her shoulders and strode through the doorway. To her credit, she didn't immediately leave. Juke pulled out her phone and checked the time. Seven hours had passed since the last incident. Why were the occurrences on a schedule? That was an invitation for a saboteur to get caught, she reasoned. Was Branx that far gone? She sighed. With Branx's knowledge of the ship, nobody was safe. Should she tell the captain? She shook her head. Without proof, her suppositions would sound like paranoid drivel. Branx was the engineering lead, and Juke herself was the lady who flew the ship. Or monkey, as much of the bridge crew affectionately called her.

The door slid open behind her, and Nin stepped out, her face pale and lips shaking. "Okay, okay," she muttered to herself.

Juke pressed her lips together. "Yeah. Not a pretty sight."

"Mr. Uxley! My bar! How could this happen?" Glizzy wailed.

"Go get cleaned up, Glizzy," Nin said. "You'll feel better with a shower and fresh clothes."

Glizzy wiped their mouth with the back of their hand and stumbled down the hall. Juke and Nin watched them go. Nin shook her head and rubbed her eyes.

"I've never seen anything like it," Juke offered.

"I don't think anything like that has ever happened, anywhere," Nin replied. "That ... that wasn't natural."

Juke sighed. She longed to tell Nin of her suspicions, her discoveries, but something stayed her. Could this phenomenon be controlled? Could Juke, herself, be a target? "What do we do, Captain?"

"I need to confer with Branx. This goes well beyond a glitch."

Juke nodded. Maybe Nin would come to the same conclusion. "Is there anything I can do?" she offered. Best to play dumb, it was what was usually expected of her anyhow. Modern ships were piloted by a machine and the crew knew it. *Just a monkey looking for her next banana, that's me*, she thought. But, would a machine care about the survival of the same crew that devalued it?

"I hate to ask, but can you go to your console and pull the logs? I want Branx scrutinizing the machinery. I want you to see if anyone was somewhere suspect. I know I can count on you to be discreet."

"I understand." Juke turned and headed to the bridge. When she was out of sight, she withdrew her phone and sent Frida a message informing her she had to work because of the incident. Incident. *What a word for it*, she thought.

*****

Juke shifted at her console, querying the computer. She had the phone codes of everyone on-board, and she could determine where they had all been in the hours before the incident. She could do this vocally, but a delicate approach would probably suit her needs better. She'd been able to screen out most of the thirty-four passengers simply by virtue of the fact they preferred to idle away time in the bar, drinking and attempting to dance. That left the crew, and the few passengers who liked to wander the ship. This wandering was not suspicious in itself, but possibly boring enough to drive someone to sabotage just to create a little excitement. The buttons chimed beneath her fingers and lights flashed in her headset. The computer, linked to her mind, was secure. There was no way to penetrate the defenses of a human mind, at least not through one of these particular models. A brilliant piece of wartime engineering.

Limiting her search to the seven hour time frame before the incident, she tracked the crew members who possessed the knowledge to sabotage the anti-gravity system. There weren't many—basically the engineering team. Most had been asleep in their quarters or in engineering, apparently working. She bit her lip. Was this line of investigation going anywhere?

The only other suspect, if it could even be called that, was a man named Lus. He had underworld connections back on Nox, and could probably have sabotage equipment on him, given his corrupt line of work. Those types could always be counted on to cause trouble. He was among those passengers who opted to stalk the halls over going to the bar. Juke checked his on-board manifest. Her cheeks reddened and her jaw dropped. Two encounters with Frida had been noted by Glizzy in security logs, but neither followed up on. So, the man was a lecher and a pervert, but that didn't make him a murderer. But so far he was the best suspect, among all those who could be ruled out. She leaned back in her chair, feeling defeated. All accounted for. Even the scumbag crime lord had checked out.

A hand suddenly grabbed her shoulder, startling her. She pulled up her visor, to see Nin looking down at her, her eyes puffy. "And?"

Juke shook her head. "Nobody out of place, no passengers with the appropriate skills were near critical systems."

"Damn."

"Now what?"

"Now, we clean up. Have engineering reconstruct the generators from the spare part stash and push as fast as we can to Elym-One. Start the calculations. Authorization to exceed speed limitations is granted."

"Got it," Juke said, pulling her visor back down. The path would take them deeper into the Molorus cluster, but empty space would be harmless at that speed. They'd already traversed the last star system, it was free and clear until they were a few light years from Elym.

Juke exhaled and began the computations. She was also planning her career change, and a new pair of boots.

Chapter 12

Hot water poured over Frida's body, coursing through her hair and steaming her face. Her eyes closed, and she tried to push the memory of the incident from her mind. The blood. So much blood. Once inside their quarters, she'd thrown her shoes in the garbage disposal and bolted for the shower. Her skin was red and angry from the scrubbing and the heat, and stung with each drop. But, she couldn't leave. It wasn't safe out there. This ship wasn't secure, and there was no way off it to safety.

"Frida?" a knock at the door announced her father's presence outside the bathroom.

She rubbed her face before answering. "Yeah?"

"You okay in there?"

"No," she admitted, looking down at the drain. In her mind's eye, it was still bloody. In reality, it was pristine.

"Come out, sweetie. Let's talk about this. I'll clean up in a bit."

Frida slowly moved to turn off the water, her skin recoiling against the cool air that rushed in the moment the heat retreated back into the faucet. Grabbing a towel, she patted her dripping skin, savoring the discomfort, allowing the sting to bring her back into reality. She donned a loose pair of cotton pants and a plain shirt. She left the bathroom, unable to meet her father's gaze, and she walked over to the sofa, sinking into the seat. Frida leaned back and stared at the ceiling, almost expecting to crash into it with no notice. Like the man in white in the bar.

Her father sat next to her, coppery scent still clinging to his skin. "That was something," he began.

"You think?"

"Space travel is not without risks." Zeke took her hand between his. "We'll get through this."

"Didn't you see that? Don't you feel?" Her face burned and she leveled a piercing stare into his eyes.

"You forget I'm three times your age. I've seen a lot, kid." He sighed. "Watching life melt on Nox as the domes went up, holding your mother as she died. Yes, I feel. All I do is feel." His eyes glistened.

"Dad, I ..." Frida began, stumbling, her anger fading into confusion.

"It's all right, just breathe."

"I don't want to die on this ship, Dad," she choked, drawing her knees up to her chest.

"You won't if I have anything to say about it. Don't think that way. A keen intellect can find a way through everything, even impossible odds."

"Yeah ..."

"How do you think I've outsmarted Lus all these years? Trust me, kid, you're better than this and you can fight."

"How can I?" she asked, unsure of how she could fight the unknown without so much as a scanner.

"Observation and analysis, just like I taught you."

"What would mom have done?"

Zeke sighed. "She'd have kept people calm. Found a way to channel their energy. Been a beacon of light and hope."

The image of her mother's face flooded her mind, eyes laced with sorrow and lips mouthing empty words. *What was she saying?* Frida wondered.

"Get some rest. Maybe Juke can give us the information we badly need to get ourselves out of this," Zeke said, rubbing her wet hair. "She's the only ally we have here, remember that. Keep her close."

Frida nodded, and climbed up to her bunk. She stared at the ceiling until the seams between the metal plates were burned into her vision. She was just a mathematician. What could she do?

***

Frida sat bolt upright as the door chimed. Zeke groaned from the bunk below her. Scrambling, she climbed down as the door chimed again. Smiling, she ran a hand through her hair. Juke was finally here! She unlocked the door, pressing the button to admit her visitor. The door slid open. Frida recoiled, it was not Juke, but Lus.

"You ..." she started, before being cut off.

"There was quite the little scene in the bar today, I heard."

"And what do you know about that?" Frida asked, scanning her mind to see if she remembered seeing him there. She'd been too engrossed in chess and Juke's arrival to remember anyone other than the man in white.

"Just that there was quite the mess. I wanted to check on you," his eyes darted to Zeke, then back to her, "to make sure you're recovering well."

"Thank you for your altruistic concern," she said. Compassion, from this monster?

"Oh, don't mistake this for mere *altruism*. I'm just here to remind you of my offer. If you need to talk, here's my contact." He slid his hand into his pocket. Frida's phone immediately buzzed.

"Thank you, but I don't think I'll be needing it."

"Your father won't be around forever, girl. You'll need a new protector soon enough. You so-called intellectuals always do," Lus hissed.

"You haven't got me yet, have you Lus?" Zeke yelled after him as Frida hit the button, closing the door in Lus' face.

"Yuck. What a piece of shit." That was her best observation.

"What a bastard, I hope he gets what's coming to him, someday. The guy is a sludge-grade fucker," Zeke said.

"What does he want with me? Why won't he leave me alone?" Frida asked, slamming the palm of her hand against the door.

"That's a story for another day," Zeke said. "For now, I suggest you stay as far away from Lus as possible. I have a feeling ..."

What feeling, Dad?"

"That this thing in the bar wasn't an accident."

Frida's leaned back against the door, elbows on knees, her face in her hands. Nobody was safe. But, could she, a theoretical mathematician, save herself, much less anyone else?

Chapter 13

Juke's nails bit into the flesh of her hands as she stood in the corridor of the eighth level, just out of sight of Frida's cabin, listening to the fragments of an echoing conversation. Someone was talking to Frida, and it didn't sound friendly. Her face flushed as she envisioned smashing whoever it was head-first into the walls, until their venomous mouth stopped spitting its poison at her lover. Pulling out her phone, she made a note of the time. The conversation had taken place in the hallway, and thus would have been recorded. Her stomach fluttered at the thought of spying, but if Frida was being threatened, she needed to be protected. For now, though, her duty to the ship forced her to obey Nin. But her care for others, and a desire to do right made her desperately want Frida's advice. Maybe, together they could figure out what the saboteur was up to, and why.

Straightening her shoulders, Juke walked through the stale air to Frida's quarters. She placed a hand against the metal door, and swallowed. Maybe she should wait. But, would waiting result in more death and damage? There was no good answer to that question. She pulled back, then her phone buzzed. Taking a moment to check it, she recoiled, dropping the device. Another incident. She was being summoned to the hall outside the bridge. Taking one longing look at Frida's door, she turned on her heel and sped down the corridor, towards the elevator.

Her mind spun and the heavy impact of her boots punctuated her thoughts. It hadn't been seven hours. It had barely been five. Her heart began to race. The horror was only just beginning. She had no choice but to talk to Nin, to do otherwise would be negligent. She didn't want to live with unnecessary deaths haunting her conscience. That wasn't something she was capable of.

She slammed her fist against the elevator's control panel. A few seconds passed, and she pounded it again and again until the door finally rattled open. Entering she rubbed her fist. She rested against the wall while the elevator shuffled her to the bridge. She furtively checked the way before leaving the lift. Wrapping her arms around her chest, Juke strode towards the site of the latest incident, steeling herself to the horrors that surely lay ahead. Pesky sprinted by her, hindquarters low and ears back. Juke didn't blame the cat. She didn't want to be here, either.

As she approached her destination, the murmurs were soon followed by the clarity of words. Deep, squeaky, both voices were raised and panicked, blending into a chorus of confounded exasperation. Nin and Branx stood with their backs to her, looking down at a wrecked anti-grav cart. A shaken crewman wrung his hands in front of him, face bloodless and upper lip shaking.

Juke fell in next to Nin, and simply listened.

"If not for damned Dumbass, I'd have been squished just like in the bar!" he said, gesturing down the hall.

"What did Pesky have to do with anything?" Branx asked.

"Cat started going batshit. Yowling, carrying on, and sprinted down the hall past me. Then ..."

"Then what?" Nin asked.

"Then I felt the wind. That thing everyone says they feel. And I ran right after that stupid cat," he said.

"That stupid cat saved your life," Nin said, examining the twisted metal.

Juke scanned the destruction. The back half of the trolley, where the generator was, had been sheared off and crushed. It was as though only a small point of the area had been affected, a singularity of chaos. She decided to test the waters. "Is there a pattern to these, captain?"

"A pattern? Since when does a malfunction have a schedule?" Branx interrupted.

Nin turned towards her. "That's your job to find out, Juke. Get going. Branx, clean this mess up and get me a report."

Juke hurried to the bridge. She could almost feel Branx's eyes burning holes into the back of her head. She may have overplayed her hand, but she had an excuse to access the ship's internal sensors. She could present her evidence, and find out what was going on with Frida at the same time.

Her stomach was a knot. How could she know she wouldn't be the next victim? Was the vessel under attack?

* * *

"What ya got for me, Juke?" Nin asked, interrupting Juke's simulations. Her mind was a mass of coordinates and times, relativity adding an extra layer of complexity to her calculations. She forced back a sigh, being interrupted while she was in a simulation was jarring and rather rude. But, this was her captain, and any insubordination would assure she would not be enjoying the rest of the voyage.

Juke forced her emotions to settle, and pulled off her visor. "Seems the events happen on a kind of schedule. The first few were exactly seven hours apart. Then, they became less than five hours apart. I'm still working out what could have changed there."

"So, you were onto something."

"Seems so. Not sure what it means yet, but I think Branx can use this to test the systems for some kind of fluctuations or malfunctions." Juke maintained eye contact. Branx would do nothing, and she knew it.

"Good. Get back to your evening, we'll reconvene in the morning," Nin said.

Juke nodded and stood up. It was time to try to help Frida with her Lus issue. *And betray the confidence of my captain and crew*, she thought.

It had to be done.

Chapter 14

The doorbell buzzed, and Frida looked up from the book she was reading on her small phone screen. She inhaled slowly, hoping it wasn't Lus again. She stood and walked to the door.

The door slid open, it was Juke's smiling face she saw. "Hello, beautiful, care for some company?" she winked twice.

Frida turned her head. It wasn't like Juke to talk in such an overtly flirtatious way. "Sure," she responded, ushering her in just as overtly.

The moment the door slid shut, Juke ran her hands through her hair and looked over her shoulder. "We need to talk. There's trouble."

Frida nodded. "More than you know." Sadly, as much as she wanted Juke to be able to dismiss him from existence, Juke could do nothing about Lus.

"I'll start. Who is Lus and why is he threatening you?" Juke crossed her arms, looking at Zeke and Frida.

Zeke shifted in his chair. "How do you know about Lus?"

"Sound travels in corridors."

Frida knit her brow and crossed her arms as well. "And you didn't come by like you said you would, why?"

"I was called to the bridge before I could come. There is somewhat of a crisis going on," Juke said. "I'm sorry if I overstepped, I just wanted to make sure you were safe."

"Don't worry about us, I've been handling that worm for longer than you've been alive," Zeke said, shaking his head. "He seems to think he is owed something."

"He's delusional," Frida spat out. "Leave it be, Juke, Dad and I can handle this. He won't be a problem forever."

"Do you think he's capable of more than just annoying young women?" Juke asked.

"I think you already know the answer to that," Zeke replied. "If you looked him up, you'd know."

Juke pursed her lips. "Do you think he's capable of sabotaging the ship?"

Frida sat bolt upright. "You mean that's what's happening to the ship? Sabotage?"

"I didn't say that," Juke replied.

"Well, if there is a saboteur they picked a terrible target. What is there to gain from random violence on a cargo ship?" Zeke asked.

"What indeed?" Juke replied.

"What do you really know, Juke?" Frida asked, her eyes pleading.

"Not much more than you do," Juke said, hanging her head low.

"Ratshit," Zeke said.

"Excuse me?"

"I think you know more than possibly everyone else on board. You're smarter than most give you credit for," Zeke said.

Juke shook her head. "I'm just the monkey who flies the ship."

"Then explain why you're here," Zeke said.

Juke took a step back, fixing her eyes to meet Zeke's gaze. Frida could tell something was off. Juke wasn't the type to hide things. "I can't say, not yet. Not without verifiable proof."

"Then you better get some. But, for your proof, Lus is capable of anything and I'd thank you to remember that in case you decide to be a hero," Zeke said.

Juke simply nodded. She didn't know how much Lus knew about her, but the way he'd talked to Frida in the hall it seemed he knew a great deal of the ship's gossip, even what was considered privy to only the crew.

"I'm glad you understand. Stay out of this matter with Lus and us, Juke. You're a good person, and it would be a shame to see something happen to you."

"Be careful, Juke," Frida said, her eyes pleading. "I know you don't want to talk about this, what you think may be going on, not yet anyway, but it's dangerous out there."

"Like we say on Nox, 'A smart man is a dead man.'" Zeke said. "So be stupid."

Juke suddenly smiled. "If there's one thing I know how to do, it's hide and look dumb."

Frida nodded. "We're here for you."

"I know," Juke said. "And thank you."

"What about the course change?" Zeke asked.

"How do you know about that?" Juke asked.

"Easy. You can feel it in the engine, and the stars slowed for a few minutes. I expect it took you a while to make the proper calculations." Zeke grinned like a man who had just put Juke's king in check.

"You are very perceptive," Juke said, before straightening. "I have to go. Got a meeting."

Frida blew her a kiss. "Come visit later, maybe we can find a way to get out of here and stretch our legs?"

"Should be safe now. Don't go out alone. Also, Pesky seems to know when something's up, listen to him. But, I didn't tell you that."

"Understood."

Juke turned and left the room. Frida and Zeke looked at each other in a moment of silence. "Think we can solve Juke's problem for her?" Frida asked.

"I'd love to try," her father replied.

Frida looked out the window, eyes drawn to the dark mass hanging in the upper right quadrant of the window. What was it? Why had they changed course again?

Were they going to be okay?

Chapter 15

Juke sprinted to her quarters, passing no one but Pesky on the way there. She manually unlocked her door, as her rooms were still technically off-limits to anyone but the engineering teams. However, she needed privacy, and the bridge was not the place to be digging for answers. The flight monkey shouldn't be the one who links the anomalies together. Something was very wrong. Sabotage, nature, or simple negligence. Which was it? How would she even know?

Picking up her books and setting them gently on her desk, she eased into her seat. There was no fear of another incident. From what she could tell, they were completely random in location on the ship. What she could determine, however, was their correlation between their points in space. The Molorus cluster had to be off-limits for a reason, right?

As the weak console in her quarters chugged away at its task, she considered the implications of feeding that small amount of information to Zeke and Frida. Would they figure it out on their own? Had she put them in danger? Was she in danger? There were too many unknowns.

Her reverie was interrupted by a beep from her console, which spat out some incomprehensible symbols and graphs. She skimmed the information, looking for something she understood. But, nothing made sense to her, the mathematics were too advanced without the aid of her computer on the bridge. Juke frowned, then straightened.

It was as though she had experienced an epiphany. She was going to get Frida and Zeke involved. Frida was the only person on the ship with the education to make sense of this without the help of a computer, and Zeke could keep her on task and offer suggestions, using his perspective and wisdom as a guide. The man could see things that most others could not.

Juke pulled out her phone and texted Frida:

[*Juke*]: I'm sending you a bunch of stuff. Do not open it until I get there.

[*Frida*]: Is it fun stuff?

[*Juke*]: You could say that, on my way to you.

Consequences be damned, she was going to figure out this problem one way or another. The worse Nin could do was fire her, right?

***

Juke was out of breath by the time she reached Frida's quarters, her thighs burning from taking the stairs instead of the lift. There was no time to wait, or to get waylaid by a meandering conversation with a crew member. She had to explain the problem to Frida, and get her focused on the case before whatever it was struck again.

Juke stood outside Frida's door, a place that was familiar by now. The curve of the hallway, the glow of the lights and staleness of the air. She hit the doorbell and waited to be admitted.

After a moment, Frida opened the sliding door and waved her in, locking the door behind her and then drawing Juke into a big hug. For a moment, the day's problems melted away with the warmth of Frida's touch. Pulling back, Juke could detect a trace of confusion in Frida's eyes, and noticed that the young woman was chewing on her lower lip.

"Hi Juke," Zeke said. "Got something to ask us?"

"You could say that. Keep in mind, talking to you could cost me my job, but I don't care anymore." Juke sank into the sofa.

"What do you mean?" Frida asked.

"This thing that's going on, I don't think it's just simple accidents. But," she looked down and sighed.

"What is it?" Zeke asked. Juke sometimes wondered if her own father could have been like Zeke, had she known him. She pushed the thought aside, her father wasn't here, and if he'd cared what happened to her she'd know who he is. Now was not the time to brood about the unknowable.

Juke set her elbows on her knees, and cradled her chin in her hands. "I pulled the data that shows where in space and when the incidents happened, but I don't understand any of it."

"What about your console on the bridge?" Frida asked.

"Nobody is taking this seriously. I think it's either a saboteur, or some phenomena."

Frida pulled out her phone and squinted. "Phenomena?"

"Listen, I can't tell you this, but the Molorus sector is forbidden, and we're in the middle of it." Juke's stomach sank. Her career was finished.

"That's a hard admission," Zeke said.

"Tell me about it. But, I'll deal with the consequences for my actions. Right now, I'll go about my duties doing whatever I'm told, while you guys try to figure out what this mess means. Are you willing to do this?"

Frida nodded, engrossed in the information on her phone.

"Thank you, Juke," Zeke said.

"What for?"

"Trusting us."

"No, you're the ones who might just save us all. I'm just the idiot who flies the ship." Juke offered Zeke a half-smile. "Now, stay in here and don't let anyone else see that. And ..."

"And?"

"The crew are not to be trusted. Nobody is is giving these incidents the seriousness that's warranted. Avoid getting into any battle of wits with engineering. Branx might be an idiot, but he's a pretty clever one."

"I see," Zeke replied. "The time has come to work, Frida. I'll cover if anyone comes to the door."

Juke's eyes stung, but she said nothing. Eleven years of her life, gone. Even among friends, the desolation tearing inside her chest was overwhelming. Perhaps all this is worth the sacrifice. What value was one woman's ordinary job compared to the lives of dozens of innocents?

A strong arm wrapped around Juke's shoulder. "You're doing the right thing," Zeke said. "For our part, we'll do our best to keep you safe. What's your phone contact, in case I need to reach you?"

Juke fumbled for her phone, and tapped it to Zeke's. The screen flashed once in confirmation. "Okay, I'll let you know if something develops, and of anything at all that might be relevant. I'd better get some sleep now before my shift starts."

Frida gave her a brief smile. "Goodnight, dear."

Juke leaned down and planted a kiss on Frida's forehead. "Stay safe. Be brilliant."

As she strode out the door, Juke knew that Frida was the right person for the task. But, it was up to Juke to watch her back until she could complete her analysis. She rubbed her palms together. They were both cold and sweaty. She couldn't just worry about Frida.

Juke had to worry about herself too.

Chapter 16

Frida pressed the buttons on her tablet like a woman possessed. There was so much to learn in order to interpret these readings. While math was essential for physics, sadly it was not the case in the inverse. Relativity, time dilation, engine dynamics, all new subjects that were to be digested before she could make any assessment of their situation. Zeke paced the length of their room while she sat cross-legged on the couch, suppressing the shivers that threatened to overwhelm her. There was a correlation, and a set amount of time between incidents.

They were due.

Any minute now, something would be smashed through the air, crushed against the ceiling or wall with blinding speed. Nothing to prepare them, other than Pesky, a slight breeze and a strange sense of malaise. Frida shuddered as she recalled that day in the bar, the presence which was outside and inside her. Seeing all, being all. But, what was it?

More button pushes. More inconclusive findings. She looked up, and stared out the window. The void had grown, occupying about half of the view. Was that the Molous sector Juke had mentioned? Frida had never considered that space could be so empty, at least inside a galaxy. However, astronomy was not her strong point, as she was quickly discovering. She put the tablet in her lap and rubbed her eyes.

"What's up, kid?"

"Nothing. Absolutely nothing. The ship is counting on me and I'm still teaching myself basic physics."

"Physics is just applied math. You've told me that a million times."

"Is that the father telling me, or the retired engineer?" she asked.

"Can it be both? Listen," he began, wetting his lips, "a problem is to be broken down into first principles. That's how physics works. Don't go for the hardest parts first, you'll just get lost. Go with what you know and build from there."

"So I'm just supposed to start easy? Juke could have done that."

"Frida, I didn't build the Hoym tunnels by telling the crews to dig from the bottom up. Trust me, you do this all the time. Your imagination has the answer already."

"My imagination isn't quantifiable," she replied.

"Isn't it? I think your body of work speaks for itself. Now, I'm going to leave you alone with the physics. Remember, Juke possibly gave up everything in her life for us to have this chance. We have to do right by her."

Frida opened her mouth to speak, but froze. Something was looking at her. Into her soul. She stared at her father, wide-eyed. He took a step back, bumping into the wall, cracking his skull against the metal in the process. The presence intensified, becoming a crackle of static electricity with a touch of heat. It was there, in the room. Frida hopped off the couch and ran to the bathroom, her heart pounding. Her father had retreated to the door, pressing his body against it, his mouth held in a toothy grimace.

It then all stopped, just as suddenly as it had began.

But how? Why?

Frida looked around. The room was undisturbed. No damage, no death. Who, or what, was that thing? What could be inside and outside of her at the same time? Could it be an alien influence, something created by the other warring faction to terrify and destroy humans? She stumbled back to her seat, pulling her knees to her chest.

Zeke sat beside her, his breath labored. A pallor had consumed his face.

"Dad?" she asked, grabbing his hand.

He faced her, mouth moving but no sound coming. His eyes bugged out, lips turning blue.

Realization struck her. She grabbed her phone, and dialed the medic. Her voice shook as she described the problem.

"I'll be right there," the voice said, before the line went dead.

Frida held her father's hand, and talked to him. Told him about all the new theories she'd learned, the beauty of science and the patterns of the universe. Appealing to his intellect, she strove to comfort him. The door buzzed soon after.

Frida sprinted to the door, slamming her hand on the button so hard it stung, leaving a white indent in the base of her palm. A tall man with dark skin and a somber expression presented at the door, followed by a shorter woman with long blond hair and a hooked nose. "Miss Juniper?" he asked.

"Yes! He's in here, please hurry!"

The two moved into their quarters with blinding speed, focused only on the almost still form of her father. The woman withdrew a scanner and ran it over the length of his body. The man pressed an electrode to Zeke's neck. "We have to move him, is that okay?"

Frida nodded, tears burning her eyes. That thing, that damned presence, had taken her father from her!

An anti-grav stretcher was shuffled into the room, and Zeke was loaded on it.

"He'll be in the sickbay. Feel free to visit in a few hours, miss."

"Yes, thank you." She ran up and kissed her dad on the cheek. "Be strong, Dad."

The door closed, leaving Frida standing, her back to the void of space. Tears streaming from her eyes, she wrapped her hands around herself to keep steady. The problem, she had to solve the problem, or things would be worse than just her father being laid up in sickbay. Everyone would be.

Now, I am alone.

Chapter 17

"Shit," Juke muttered under her breath, sitting in the bridge's break room with her phone held to her chest. Her hand squeezed the device, and the overwhelming need to pitch it against the window threatened to overrule her reason. She sucked in several deep breaths to center herself. It was hard enough to pretend everything was fine and that she suspected nothing, but it was altogether another thing to lose one of the few allies she had. She re-read Frida's text:

[*Frida*]: It got Dad, he's in sickbay.

[*Juke*]: Are you okay?

[*Frida*]: I have to be. I'll go visit him when I'm allowed.

[*Juke*]: I'll be with you as soon as I can. Be strong.

Tears threatened to force their way out of her eyes. How could she just tell Frida to be strong? The woman's father was gravely ill, and she was being expected to do calculations. It was so callous. So selfish. *Damnit, Juke,* she thought. Why did it have to be like this? Zeke was the key, a guiding light in all this. Someone with the perspective to keep the tendrils of fear from their hearts. Would he recover? Could that monster Lus take advantage and strike when the man had no ability to protect himself?

"Juke." Juke startled, and turned around. It was Nin.

"Yes, captain?" she asked, rising from her seat.

"We're getting more turbulence. Make sure to even out the drive fields in navigation when you get back from your break."

Juke nodded. "I'll take care of it." She slid her phone back into her pocket.

Nin pursed her lips, her eyes roaming over Juke's face. "Is everything okay?"

"I'm just recovering from the bar incident. I don't like the sight of blood," she said.

"Nor do I. Let's hope for a clean end to our voyage. Enjoy your break." Nin turned, leaving the small room. Juke stood, and watched her go. The woman she'd trusted with her life for eleven years. The person she suspected of not caring if Juke lived or died. It was a difficult duality to accept.

Was it even her captain at all? she wondered, surprised by the sudden thought. Nin was usually warm, concerned, and empathetic. Fun. Now, she seemed to care more about her time lines than safety. Reckless. It was odd.

Juke sat back down, and resumed watching the stars. Her stomach was a hollow pit, and her mind a racing mess. The loss of control panicked her—that's why she liked to fly the ship. That control, that power. It was her responsibility to keep the others safe, rather than hope some hapless grunt didn't land them in a black hole.

A black hole?

She whipped out her phone and texted Frida:

[*Juke*]: Could it be a black hole?

The buzzer on her phone went off, signaling the end of her break. She stood, stretching her back and headed back to her console. She smiled at the others as she took her station, and went back to harmonizing the drive fields with the engine frequencies. Mindless work, but it would pass the time until she could see Zeke and Frida. They were safer together. At least she hoped they would be.

***

Juke pushed back from her desk, the tension behind her eyes easing as she turned her attention away from the screen. The hum of the engine fluctuated slightly, but the turbulence had mostly been settled. She'd spent over an hour tackling the problem. A few crew members milled around, working and ignoring her. The door to Nin's office was locked, indicated by the red light on the wall. Juke booked it out of there, throwing her legs as far and fast as they could move. She bit her tongue as she walked to the lift, willing herself to be invisible. Don't see me, don't talk to me, let me end my day.

The door slid open, and she stepped inside. Her shoulders slumped as the scrutiny of the crew sloughed off of her. She pulled out her phone. Frida hadn't responded.

[*Juke*]: Where are you? I'm done.

The elevator stopped at level three. Pocketing the phone, she stepped out. Sickbay was to the left. Crew had priority, so she could see Zeke. Maybe Frida would be with him.

A breeze eased its way down the hall, and the invisible eyes were again upon her. The engine thrummed and lurched. Something was inside her, a presence that was knowing yet unfamiliar. Was it alive? Could she speak to it, reason with it?

Juke opened her mouth, but as she began to speak the presence had vanished, leaving behind still, metallic air and a lonely ship. She rounded the corner, almost tripping over Pesky, who was semi-cloaked in the dim light. The cat yowled at her, and sprinted past. Juke stood still, watching the cat go. Could the cat see something they couldn't? *Perhaps I can check the sensors later, and track Pesky. Damn thing has to register on the internal life-signs, right?* Juke thought.

Juke resumed her walk to sickbay. Bile rose at the back of her throat, and her nose wrinkled. What was that smell? The ship scrubbed all particulates from the atmosphere. It should hold no scent.

"Oh, shit," Juke groaned, before doubling over, emptying the contents of her stomach on the metal floor. The loose yellow slurry mixed with the spreading pool of blood. She stumbled back, her legs failing her as she fell hard onto her back. Air expelled from her lungs, and she couldn't force it back in. She opened her eyes.

Above her, the ceiling dripped with blood. Patches of short brown hair were clinging to it. The wall and floor was awash in gore. Offal and intestines twisted together into an unholy mound straight from a horror vid. It was a scene beyond any nightmare. And the blood, it didn't stop. It wouldn't stop moving.

It was coming for her.

Juke screamed, shuffling backwards. *Have to get away from it, have to get away.*

After a few meters, the blood slowed, glistening black in the dull light. Nothing moved. Juke's mind raced, and she pulled her phone from her pocket and signaled the emergency alert at her location. Then, she lay back on the floor, knees up but eyes fixed on the lights above her. The glare caused spots to dance in her eyes. Juke didn't care. It was better than seeing anything else. Ever again.

Frida.

Juke checked her phone, and texted her, telling Frida to stay away from the hallways outside of sickbay. She can't see that, not again. Juke had signed up for this duty. Frida was only a passenger, someone to be protected and sheltered.

Heavy footfalls echoed down the corridor. Crashing to a halt, they were replaced by curses, gasps, and prayers. "Juke?" one asked. It was the medic, Verus, crouching over her and taking her hand.

"Yeah, it was so fucked up, like… shit," she said.

"Go rest in your quarters. Write your report and recover. I'll take over from here," he said. Verus's dark eyes misted, but the deep compassion of his voice could never be mistaken for fake.

Juke nodded, and let Verus help her. Strong hands hauled her to her feet. "Do you need someone to walk you back?" he asked.

Juke shook her head. "Thank you, Verus," she said.

She wasn't going back to her quarters.

Chapter 18

"Damn it, damn it, damn it!" Frida shouted, her voice reverberating off the walls of her quarters. She couldn't see her dad, and if she spent one more minute in this tin can of a room she was going to explode. She hadn't slept, barely eaten, and all she could do was stare at numbers. Juke had suggested a black hole. Unlikely. She needed her father, she needed Juke. Even Pesky would help, the stupid beast. "Make it make sense!" She was ready to throw her tablet across the room.

Her phone buzzed. She checked it and made a face. Lus. She put her phone back in her pocket and resumed pacing. Natural, artificial, intelligent, automated. She'd covered so many possibilities. From what she could research, there had been no phenomena like this ever before. But, humans had been to the Molorus sector. There had to be a recorded reason why it was forbidden, right?

Her phone signaled her attention, again. She ignored it. Nothing was getting in the way of her work. Secretly, she hoped Lus would be the next to have his head smashed against the ceiling. The man had it coming, and she was beyond the point of caring about what that secret hope said about her character. He'd threatened her, Juke, and her father. He had enslaved and tormented thousands. And, he was creepy. Most damning of all, he was responsible for the death of her mother. But enough. He was also a distraction from her task. And how did she know he wasn't the one behind it all?

She plinked at a few buttons. If nothing physically lifted them, and there was nothing wrong with the artificial gravity, then what could it be? If not something allowed by the laws of physics, then perhaps she should turn to the simple, comforting, realm of pure mathematics for answers? How could something get inside a closed room without going in through a window or door? There had to be a way.

The door buzzed. She ignored it, and resumed her pacing. In, in, in. How could something get in?

Again, the buzzer. She wished she could see who it was. Sighing, she locked her tablet with a complex algorithm only she knew the code to and walked to the door, holding the tablet tightly to her chest. After pausing for a moment, she opened the door.

Juke stood before her, shaking, and her face was a mask of death, her skin a pallor. A strange coppery smell accompanied her, a smell that Frida knew, but couldn't quite place.

"Juke! Are you okay!"

Juke shook her head. "Can I come in?" she asked, stammering.

Frida stepped out of the way, taking care to lock the door once Juke had crossed the threshold. "Can I get you some water?"

"Yeah," Juke said as she sank into the couch.

Frida walked to the food dispenser and ordered a glass of cold ice water. It was her favorite non-bar drink. The water on Nox had never tasted this good. She handed the glass to Juke and then sat and turned to face her. "What happened? You look like shit!"

Juke contemplated the glass before bringing it to her lips. Her hands were trembling. Frida wrapped her hands around the glass, steadying it. "Another incident."

Another? They were getting closer together, this one a mere three hours after the past. "We'll figure this out. I'll get to the bottom of it." *I hope.*

"Yeah, just outside sickbay."

"You saw it?" Frida asked.

"I found the poor bastard." Juke said, her color changing to a more greenish hue. Frida knew what that meant.

"Oh, hells, I'm so sorry Juke." Seeing it happen once was bad enough, but randomly walking into piles of viscera was almost worse than she could handle. Frida wrapped her arms around Juke, and squeezed hard. What else could she do?

"Yeah, listen, I think Pesky might be a clue," Juke said, locking eyes with her.

"How could that be? He's just a cat."

"I'm not sure how, but he seems to be able to detect this… entity…I guess… before we can. Like heightened senses. Maybe if I scan near where he was during the incidents, I can find a clue. I don't know. I barely know my own name anymore." Juke said with a sigh.

"Like, his more feral instincts kicking in and giving him an awareness we humans no longer possess?" Juke asked, her focus returning.

"You're right, he's just a cat. Forget I mentioned it." Frida paused, her mind working. "No, I need to check a few things. You might have just given me an idea." It was a long shot, but desperation was a good motivator.

"Can I help? I have a responsibility to this ship." Juke's voice was regaining some of its lost strength, and the determination that Frida found so intoxicating was finding its way back into Juke's gaze.

"Get me Pesky's coordinates," Frida said. "As for the rest, let me take care of it."

"Nerd."

Frida shrugged. "It's what you fell for!"

Chapter 19

Juke's stomach churned as she sat at the console in her forbidden quarters. She knew she shouldn't be in there, but she had to do this. Pesky couldn't talk, so the sensors would be his voice. She acquired the data, and sent it to Frida before scrubbing her queries from the computer's memory. If Juke was discovered and they lived, well, she'd prefer not to consider a career in manual labor or becoming an accountant. *Ugh, numbers that aren't vectors or tensors*, she thought.

She snuck out of her quarters, relieved that nobody was in the hall. Acting natural was the last thing she wanted or could do, but the mind could perform amazing feats under duress. In her hand, she held her phone, set to scanning mode. She was going to find Pesky, the little shit, and follow him around. She wanted to monitor how he behaved. If cats could be normal. This one was nicknamed *Dumbass* after all. Her mind ruminated over the additions she had made recently to her resume: spy, insubordinate, paranoid, obsessed. She concluded, however, that she'd rather be all that, and worse, than dead. It was simply a matter of perspective.

Level four section six, came the reading. She high-tailed it then, walking as fast as she could while still taking the time to cordially acknowledge those she encountered on her way. Pretending to text, she kept her head low. She barely heard the footsteps as they sped up behind her, a deep voice clearing and announcing a man's presence. Juke pocketed her phone before looking at her new companion. Lus.

"Can I help you?" she asked. Scum though he was, part of her job was helping the passengers if they needed something.

"Indeed," he said, matching her pace. "I understand you are acquainted with the Juniper family?"

Juke ground her teeth and balled her hands into fists. "I have had the opportunity to make their acquaintance, yes. Are you friends with them?"

Lus offered up cruel eyes with his toothy grin. "You could say that I'm a very old friend of Zeke's."

"I see, what can I do for you?" More information was good information, even if she'd need to bathe three times after this conversation to clear the man's leering slime off her soul.

"I need you to send a message to Frida. I understand you have her ear." He licked his lips.

Juke fought down the need to punch his teeth out and wear them as a necklace. "What is it? She's busy."

"Tell her that uncle Lus needs to talk to her about business ... and pleasure."

"Is that all?"

"I suggest leaving well enough alone with them. That family brings trouble, and I hate to see anything happen to such a promising young woman such as yourself."

"Noted. I'll deliver your message when I see her," Juke said flatly.

"One more thing," Lus purred.

Juke held back a plethora of rude gestures and comments. "Yes?"

"Wish old Zeke a speedy recovery. Pity what happens when you least expect it."

Juke nodded, and with that Lus was gone. Her face became flushed and her heart pounded out a hard rhythm. He was threatening Frida! Worse still, did he have anything to do with Zeke's condition? It was unthinkable to have that slimy creature on board during this crisis. Even Pesky had more decency, and he didn't always use the litter box. Maintenance had been complaining about the little shit for years. *Joke's on them, that little jerk might save us all*, she thought.

***

Pesky rolled onto his back, inviting her with the forbidden temptation of his soft belly. Juke knew better and simply glowered at him. "Come on cat, let's go for a walk or something," she said. Stupid thing. Pesky eventually flipped to his feet and started walking, ambling down the hall with no real direction or intent. Juke followed, and resumed scanning. This time, she was trying to view Pesky's life signs. She longed for a real tool from sickbay, but that would open her up to suspicion. Plus, who wants to monitor the captain's cat? *Evidently, me*, she thought. *Maybe I really am the ship's monkey.*

She watched the timer. Something should happen, any moment. The anomaly appeared like clockwork, causing destruction everywhere it went. She kept quiet, doing her best to keep Pesky's senses as unstimulated as possible. Her phone's processing power was limited to the extent that even sound could throw off the measurements.

While Juke was considering getting a more modern phone, Pesky froze. His back arched and his tail puffed up. With a start, he ran off down the hall. Juke sprinted after him, barely aware of the presence taking hold inside of her. The air moved around her, her ponytail lifting toward the ceiling. "No!" she screamed, running faster. The entity watching her, hunting her, grew weaker and the wind dissolved to stillness. Pesky was nowhere to be seen. Juke's heart raced and she bent over, panting, gasping for air. The goosebumps on her arms lowered. It was like nothing had happened.

It had come for me.

Juke couldn't believe it. Was Pesky somehow a catalyst for the attacks?

It came for me!

She turned on her heel and sprinted for the stairs. She had to tell Frida. Everything.

Could something be hunting us?

Chapter 20

Pounding with the urgent ringing of the doorbell interrupted Frida's thoughts. Frida straightened. Who couldn't just use the doorbell and wait? Juke, of course. Shaking her head, she stood, stretching her legs before moving toward the noise. She was a mess—hair disordered, clothes slept in, and hadn't eaten a proper meal in days. She was running on sugar and sheer determination. It was like being a student, but in space and with people dying. Nowhere near as many parties, either. What she wouldn't give for a glass of orange juice, or something Glizzy dreamed up. No word from sickbay. No word from Juke. There was just her, and whatever horrible formula she'd just derived.

She opened the door to find Juke, her spiking every which way, wild eyed and breathing hard. "Let me in!" she said.

Frida waved her in before locking the door. This was getting to be a habit. "Damn, you look terrible! What's happened?"

"I feel worse than I look. It almost got me."

Frida's mouth dropped open. "What?"

"I was following Pesky, just to scan his activity."

"Scanning cats, is this how you spend your off hours?" Frida asked.

"Someone I'd rather spend time with is trying to save the ship, so yes." Juke sank down into the sofa, curling up in the corner.

"What happened?" Frida asked, rolling her shoulders. All her calculations were driving her into an information overload. Her mind was beginning to cloud over, but she willed it back into service.

Juke explained the Pesky freak out, the wind, the anti-gravity effect and the presence. How strong it was. The lightness of her body and the floating hair. Outrunning it and getting away as fast as she could. "I think it's hunting us," she concluded.

Frida remained silent, her mind working. What hunted by smashing people into the ceiling? What was the deal with Pesky always being around, did cats draw invisible anti-gravity monsters to them?

"One other thing," Juke said.

"Yeah?"

"I ran into your uncle Lus."

Frida threw her head back. "No relation, I assure you." She wanted to scream.

"He wants to meet with you, and implied a few things about Zeke's illness I'd rather not repeat."

Frida's vision went red. "That rat! I'll get him for this myself!"

Juke took Frida's hand and pulled her onto the couch. "He's not worth it, let's just solve this thing before anyone else gets hurt. But, Frida?"

"Yes?" Frida had already pulled out her tablet and was tapping away.

"Can I stay here? I don't want to be alone."

Frida looked over at Juke, noting the misty eyes and pinched lips. They needed to stick together, it would be safer that way. "Absolutely. We're better off together."

Juke's smile only graced the edges of her lips. She climbed to the top bunk, where she lay down without adjusting the blankets.

"I'm gonna rest before my shift. Wake me up if you get news about your dad, okay?"

"You got it." Frida quickly took out her phone, and pinged sickbay. It had been hours. A request for an update couldn't hurt, right? She needed her father, and she was close to solving this. So close. The answer was in the math, and math was all she was really good at.

***

Frida's phone buzzed, and she rubbed her bleary eyes. She must have nodded off. Opening it, she saw a message that her father was stable, and available for visitors. She heaved a sigh of relief —at least something was going right. She stood up, head spinning for a moment while she righted herself. Stifling a yawn, she walked over to the bunk bed and climbed to the top, shaking Juke awake. "Hey, we can go see my dad," she said.

Juke's eyes fluttered open, and she turned over, inching herself out of the bed. "First good news I've had in a while. Want to go?"

"Yes. I think I have a theory. It's totally bogus, but it fits the facts of what's going on."

Juke offered a tight smile. "That's great, you'll tell me about it, right?"

"When we're with Dad. Can you kick the medics out for privacy?" Frida asked.

"I'll see what I can do."

***

Sickbay was a sterile plane of light, as opposed to the gloom of the rest of the ship. Three beds sat against the far wall, each separated by a flimsy white curtain. There was a terminal at the foot of each bed, and two plastic white desks at the front of the room. There were other doors on the room's sides, but they were closed. Frida didn't care what was in there. There was only one reason she was in sickbay, and that was her dad. She scanned the beds. Only one was occupied, and she saw him lying the far right one, eyes closed and a yellow force field dancing over his body. "Dad ..." she said, walking towards him.

"Would you care to sign in, miss? Hello, Juke." The medic stepped out of one of the rooms and looked them over, leaning against the wall. The heavy circles under the eyes spoke of unforgettable horrors and disaster.

Frida drew back for a moment. "Yes, of course." She took the offered pen and scribbled down her name, checking the time.

"You got lucky. I don't have the equipment to do a full scan on him, but we're keeping him in stasis until we arrive at Elym. They'll be able to treat him there."

Frida rushed to her father's side, grabbing his big hand. It was cold to the touch. He had the semblance of a corpse. Still and unbreathing, he was there, trapped in time.

Trapped in time. But, if you could be trapped in time, could you be trapped in space?

Frida dropped his hand. "We have to go. I think I understand."

"What, Frida, it's your dad!"

"And he just gave me the last piece of the puzzle. Now let's go!"

Frida ran out the door, tailed closely by Juke. It all made sense. It was insane, but it made sense.

Chapter 21

Their feet thudded down the hall, running as fast as they could to get away from Pesky. People died when he was around, and they weren't about to be next. Frida had insisted on absolute secrecy. There was no knowing what she saw when she had looked at her father's still body, but something in her consciousness had seen beyond the carnage and horror and into the workings of the universe itself. Juke could kiss her right now, but the sense of being watched came over them.

"Not again!" Juke yelled. "Faster, Frida!"

Frida pumped her arms harder in response, her breath coming in ragged pants.

She couldn't let Frida die—she was the only one with the key. Juke tensed her muscles, preparing for one final act of bravery. Steeling herself, she got ready to push Frida free of their pursuer at the cost of herself. *But I don't want to die, either*, she thought.

The wind came, tearing at their hair, stronger than the last time Juke had felt it. The thing was seeing out of their eyes, perhaps even hearing through their ears. What could it be? Where was it? Was the floor itself evil?

Then, just as suddenly as it had begun, the winds ceased. Their boots returned to their hard banging on the ground and they slowed, if only for a moment. "Go," Juke gasped.

"No," stammered Frida, her breathing coming in short spasms.

Juke knew she had to get Frida back to her quarters, somewhere to recover. It wasn't far. "Just a few more feet ... you," she said, before her lungs failed her.

They came to Frida's quarters and threw themselves through the portal, doubling over and heaving as though no amount of air on the ship could still their gasps. Juke pulled Frida to the sofa, and they sat. Juke's legs cramped and shook. It was almost time for her shift. Going outside alone terrified her, but if it was possible to save the ship from the bridge then she'd do it.

"Okay, Frida ... tell me."

Frida pressed a few buttons on her tablet. "I got the idea when I saw my dad. You know how stasis is like locking something in time?"

Juke nodded. That was about all she knew about the subject.

"So, I think what's happening is we've become trapped in space."

What? "But, we're still moving, Frida. I fly the damn ship! We can't be trapped in space." That defied the very concept of space, didn't it? To be moving and in stasis defied logic.

"But we're in a different kind of space, that's what I mean," Frida replied.

"There are more than one kind of space? How the hells does that work?"

"Well, think of it this way. We live in three dimensions, right?"

Juke nodded. "Well, yeah. That's how we get around."

Frida paced the length of the room, touching the top of her tablet to her chin, lecturing. "However, what if we flew into a place where there was a fourth? We would have no way of knowing."

Juke shook her head. "That's crazy," she said.

"Hear me out, Juke. A three dimensional object can enter two dimensional space without going through any of the lines, right?" Frida's eyes were lit up with an intensity Juke had never seen before. Her voice locked Juke's attention, holding her rapt and agog.

"Sure? If you say so?" Juke really had no idea.

"A four dimensional object, by that logic, could enter our space without going through any window or door. It would just appear."

"I see. Sorta."

"Don't you get it?" Frida asked. "We managed to fly into a forbidden part of space, which is probably forbidden for this very reason. Now, something from the fourth dimension is hunting us."

"More like hunting Pesky."

"Still a problem, Juke."

"So, if you're right, we just have to leave this dimension area type thing and we'll be okay?"

"I think it's more of a hypersphere, but yes."

"A what?"

"It's a four dimensional sphere. Every point on the inside is a point on the surface."

"Okay ..." Juke sighed. *Why did it have to be math?* "So why don't I just fly us out of here?"

"I don't know where it ends," Frida said, turning her gaze to the floor.

"You better figure it out," Juke said. "I gotta get to work. Ping me when I can go to the captain with this."

"I will," Frida said, waving as she left.

Juke began walking to the bridge, not caring that she was wearing the same clothes as yesterday. It was time to put this insanity to bed.

Chapter 22

"Hey, Juke, lookin' good!" Branx announced in front of the entire bridge crew. Juke's cheeks heated. She hadn't even brushed her hair. Slumping into her chair, she tried not to be seen. "Bet you had a great time last night. Your little friend again?"

Juke wanted to shove him out the airlock, or send him to pet Pesky. Whichever was easier. His needling inflamed something in her, something intolerable and needing to explode. "At least I get some, Branx. When's your voice gonna break?"

"Bitch."

"Okay, that's enough," Nin's deeper voice clearly pierced the din of their argument, stopping them in their tracks. Juke turned back to her station and went silent. She wanted off this damn ship. But not before she found a way to murder Branx.

"Juke, make sure you're dressed properly for duty in the future," Nin said.

"Understood."

"Branx, don't be a dick. Don't you have work to do?"

"I thought inspecting the ship was my work, captain," he replied.

Juke bit her lip. Branx may not be smart enough to be a saboteur after all. If it were like Frida said, and they'd just wandered into the Molorus sector, then it was nobody's fault but the captain's, right?

"The engines are out of alignment. Again. Get to engineering. Now." Nin's voice held a hard edge to it, one tired and tight.

Branx turned and left the bridge without another word. At least Juke didn't have to endure another instance of his squeaky voice or beady eyes. *Pervert.*

Juke plugged away on her console, ignoring the murmuring voices that intermingled on the bridge. There was an emptiness inside her. Sitting still at a console seemed to be a death sentence. She couldn't run away on the bridge. She couldn't escape. She was helpless. Stuck here with people who were oblivious to the real nature of the threat.

Juke's phone buzzed. She excused herself to go on break. When she opened the message, her eyes popped. Frida had sent her all the proof she needed, and was working on the course to take them out of this hypersphere thing. Her stomach knotted. It was time to brief Captain Nin, but Juke wasn't exactly in the captain's good graces at the moment. For some reason, Nin favored the engineer.

Juke walked through the bridge and buzzed on the door to the captain's office. A ping admitted her, and she stepped inside. Nin's office was a stark contrast to the rest of the ship. It was warm, wood paneled and plush, with shelves of memorabilia and certificates on the wall. Nin sat at a black desk. She switched the computer off and leveled a steady gaze at Juke. "Yes?"

Juke licked her dry lips. "Captain, I think I know what's happening to the ship."

"Better than Branx?"

"Branx is an idiot. He's probably still chasing sensor ghosts and rebuilding the anti-grav system." Juke didn't hold back this time. She knew she was finished on this ship, so she may as well air her grievances.

Nin frowned, knitting her brow and crossed her arms. "Go on, then."

"I've been doing some research and tracking of the anomalies. Who is around, what happens, how long. You know, general diagnostics you asked me to do," Juke said.

Nin nodded. This caused Juke to sweat and the hairs on the back of her neck to stand at attention.

"And, I think these incidents is linked to the area of space we're in. The Molorus cluster. It has to be off-limits for a reason, right?"

"No, there is no reason. This is just an area of space with nowhere to stop if there's trouble."

"Like now?"

"Don't question me like that." Nin glared at Juke, lips tugged downwards.

"I'm sorry, captain. Can I finish my report?"

Nin leaned back in her chair and sighed. "Go ahead."

Juke swallowed, and pulled out her phone, lighting up the projector screen on the wall. It contained Frida's calculations and hypothesis, completely illustrated and annotated. At the end, Juke stopped speaking and looked at Nin expectantly.

"An interesting theory. Tell me, who helped you with it?"

Juke looked at her feet. "Frida and Zeke Juniper."

"Two of the passengers?" Nin jumped to her feet. "You gave sensitive data to some passengers?"

"Frida's a mathematician! She can see things we can't. She was the only one I could trust." Juke sighed.

"You couldn't bring this to Branx?" Nin tugged on a strand of hair.

"Branx spends more time speculating on my love life than doing his job, captain. How was I to know it wasn't his negligence?"

"Tread carefully, Juke."

"I just wanted to help. This thing keeps happening. It almost caught me, twice! I want to live. Fire me if you need to, but know that I just wanted everyone to get to Elym safely." Juke clasped her hands in front of her face. "I don't want to die, Nin. I don't want to see some other human get splattered again."

Nin shook her head and drew herself to her feet. "Okay, Juke. I get it. So… what exactly does Frida suggest we do about it?"

"She's calculating the fastest way out of the hypersphere as we speak."

"Where is she?"

"In her quarters, where she's safer."

"Take me to her. Now."

Juke could only nod, her heart racing in her chest. This wasn't good. Frida had no warning, and no idea what kind of Hell she was getting into with Nin.

Chapter 23

Frida answered the door, wearing only a long t-shirt. It had been a long night, and her diet of snack food had left her too bloated for her pants to feel comfortable. It would just be Juke again, though she'd be hours early. Maybe there was news? Instead, Captain Nin loomed over her, Juke standing behind her to the left. Frida's squeaked and she ran back into her room. "Just a minute!" *This is terrible, I met the captain and I don't even have pants on. What a nightmare.* Pulling on a pair of white pants, she rushed back to the door. "Apologies, can I help you?" Juke's face looked like she was struggling to keep from laughing.

"Frida Juniper, I presume?" Captain Nin asked, her voice oozing authority.

Frida nodded, her face still red. "Please, come in, Captain. My apologies again, I wasn't prepared for visitors."

Nin stepped into the room with the gravitas of a captain. Her eyes took in everything, and appeared to see through Frida, past any mask she might be wearing. "Tell me what you've found. Juke gave me a report, but I need it from you." Nin smiled, but the lines did not reach her eyes. Frida held in a shudder. Her stomach squirmed, the feeling like she's done something wrong or illegal crawled across her skin.

"You see, my calculations indicate that we've wandered into an area of space that contains what theoretical mathematicians refer to as a *hypersphere*," Frida began, her voice slipping easily into the cadence and tone of an academic giving a lecture. "This means that something that exists in this fourth dimension is able to enter our space, but without going through any of our windows or doors. Kind of like how we can enter a drawn two dimensional object without putting our finger through the lines. But, there's a way we can protect ourselves," she added. "It's not easy, but this presence thing has a limit, one we lack. With some strategy on our side, and clear communication and steady command I think we can minimize further damage."

"There is?" Juke exclaimed.

"We simply have to keep moving."

"What exactly does that accomplish, Frida?" Nin asked.

"The phenomenon is confined to the surface of the construct, and has to move around the hypersphere to reach us. If we all keep moving around inside the ship, whatever it is can't get an exact fix. All of its victims were standing still, right?"

Nin nodded. "Apparently so, according to Juke's analysis. So, where do we need to get to to get out of this damned thing, then?" Nin practically spat the words out of sheer exasperation. Hypersphere, fourth dimension, it was all a bit much to compute on short order.

"I'm figuring that out. But, I know we must be close to the center. That's why the attacks are getting closer together."

"Suggestions?" Nin asked.

"Get everyone moving? Nobody stays still until we're clear. It's hard, but it could save lives."

"But, that might take days! You're proposing everyone on this ship, crew and passengers alike, abandon their rooms, posts and avoid using the toilet?" Nin said, incredulous.

"I also suggest locking Pesky up in a cargo bay. Your cat seems to be a focal point of the attacks."

Nin touched her forehead. "Okay, Pesky does some hard time in solitary and I'll have all systems set to autopilot."

Frida stood still, uncertain of what to say.

"You two, get moving. I'll deal with the rest. Can you compute and walk at the same time, Frida?"

Frida held up her tablet. "And I can run with scissors, too," she offered.

"Go," Nin said with a half-smile. "And Juke?"

"Yes?" Juke looked up at her commander.

"Get out of my sight."

Juke and Frida walked out the door, taking care to head in the opposite direction of Captain Nin. Juke squeezed Frida's arm, and Frida pinged Aesop, the ship's AI, to have it help with the final computations. She felt so close to the solution, and yet so far. If more people died, it would be on her. All she wanted to do was sleep.

***

"Attention all crew and passengers," Nin's voice came through the speakers with a crisp authority, echoing down the halls of the ship. Juke and Frida had made it to the fifth level, their legs aching from climbing so many stairs. The lifts didn't seem like a good idea, but they didn't want to stay on the same deck. "You are hereby ordered to vacate your quarters and present locations and move around the ship until ordered otherwise. This is a matter of life or death. This phenomena can strike those who stand still, and as such the ship will be placed on auto pilot until we can determine the best course of action. I repeat, do not stop moving, no matter the cost." There was an audible click, and the hallway returned to its dull humming.

"Well, that's just great," Juke said.

"What do you mean?" asked Frida.

"If the ship is on autopilot, who is going to enter the new coordinates?" Juke shook her head. "This makes no sense."

"Aren't you the pilot? Can't the computer do it?" Frida's gut gurgled, protesting against the days of junk food and sudden activity.

"Aesop isn't for navigation. It's a safety design feature so we don't get sent into a star by some malicious force. Like by the Kijh, the alien bastards love those kinds of tricks," Juke laughed, but the humor of it was lost on Frida. How could flying into a star make Juke laugh? She lived in space. "Now we're having a problem of the opposite order. We need a remote control and we're stuck pacing the ship."

Frida pressed a few more buttons on her tablet, frowning. So close. Maybe another hour. If she could make it that long without needing the lavatory. "So, how are we supposed to go to the bathroom?"

"Damned if I know, but I expect the ship is gonna be pretty gross by the time we're done." Juke made a face. "Hope you can breathe through your mouth."

"Nasty," Frida said, pulling a face.

"Say, Frida," Juke began, "how did you get into all this esoteric stuff?"

Frida shrugged. "After my mom died, I did a lot of puzzles, kid puzzles, but all the same. Stuff to distract myself, make the pain go away. Dad helped, taught me chess."

Juke nodded. "So you feel better with that focus?"

"You could say that. Concentration and a task keep my mind away from fixating on the loss, and the reality of being stuck on Nox-Gamma for life." Frida's voice wobbled a bit, but she tried to hold it together. Now wasn't the time to have a breakdown.

"I see. I felt a similar way with navigation and art. The barrens of my home planet became less desolate when I surrounded myself with beauty, and the ability to get away ...forever."

"Do you want to escape from your life here?" Frida asked, pressing a few buttons.

Juke nodded. "My career on this ship is over. This place is all I've known for eleven years." She sniffed and rubbed her left eye.

Frida took her tablet in one hand and briefly rubbed Juke's shoulder. "Juke?"

"Yes?"

"Run away to Elym with Dad and me. We can all start over, build a real life with real things." For the first time in her life, Frida wanted the real thing. Not just another symbol or number. A reality beyond mere existence, beyond mathematics.

"I thought you preferred the abstract?"

"So do you, Juke. We can be conceptual together." Frida sighed. "Speaking of concepts ..."

An alarm went off, shattering Frida's train of thought. The lights in the hallway flashed red every few seconds. The now-familiar chill of the entity was with them, raising the fine hairs on their skin and seeing through their eyes. Weaker than before, they picked up the pace, power walking down the hallway. "An alarm?" Juke asked.

"Maybe the engineer was able to figure out how to detect it," Frida offered. "In theory, my data could do that, but I had no access to the ship's systems."

"Makes sense."

The presence dissipated, the air returned to its canned stillness and the lights returned to their sickly orange hue. "Okay, I'll let Aesop chew on that for a few minutes. I think we're good to just wander a bit." She took Juke's hand. "Tell me what you'd do with a new life."

Chapter 24

Screaming echoed along the halls of level ten. The child's cries pierced Juke's ears and quickened her breath. The wailing came again. The bottom of the ship probably had a few people in it, even though the halls had become progressively more crowded. Outside Glizzy's bar had been the worst—the expelled drunken idiots they so loved to watch dance stumbled, holding the walls and desperately trying to keep moving without soiling themselves. It would be comical if they weren't all in danger. "Frida, let's save that kid! He's in trouble!"

They took off at a run, navigating around a few people they'd found meandering the hallways. Juke's already aching leg muscles protested the activity. They had been walking for over three hours, staying alert for when the next attack would come.

They found a little boy, the bottoms of his jeans soaked in blood, running from a pile of viscera that could only have been one of his parents. It was impossible to tell which one. Could the hair plastered to the ceiling be long, and black? Juke didn't look, she turned her attention to the boy, his cherubic face stained with tears. He could only have been four years old, if that, and Juke knew she had to do something. Swooping down, she scooped the child up in her arms, and turned on her heel. "Come on, upstairs," she barked at Frida.

Frida didn't waste any time in turning and following Juke. They marched to the stairs, intending to walk up to the ninth floor. "Where do we go?" she asked. The little boy squirmed and wailed in her arms, but Juke held him fast, tight against her hip.

"Let's keep him with us. When we get out of here we can take him to sickbay so the medics can look after him." Juke figured medics knew about kids—she certainly didn't. "What's your name, little guy? I'm Juke, and this is Frida."

The kid continued to wail, struggling against her grip. Juke shot a pleading glance to Frida, whose eyes widened in response. Juke suspected child rearing was not part of math class. Juke stroked his hair, spoke softly in his ear, and held his small body close. She didn't know what else to do, but getting him away from the carnage was a good first step. Her shoulder grew wet with his tears and snot and she needed to re-adjust her grip several times. But, she could not dare to put him down—that would place them all in danger. So hold on she did, hoping he would tire himself out. "Think he has another parent here?" Frida asked.

"I don't usually look over the passenger manifests, that's not part of my job. If you want to take him for a minute I can contact security."

Frida swallowed, and then held out her arms. Taking the kicking and screaming child into her arms, she began cooing and mumbling in his ear, oblivious to the bloodstains forming where his shoes hit her white pants. "Okay, I got him."

Juke withdrew her arms, and reached for her phone. Dialing the head of security, she waited for an answer.

"Security," a deep voice answered. It must be Delkin, he was usually the one who responded first. Kazik was way too important to lower himself to answering calls.

"Delkin, can you check the passenger manifests? We found a child on level ten and we need to see if he has," she paused, considering her words. Best just to spit it out. "Another parent."

"I see. Let me check, What does he look like?"

Juke looked at the boy momentarily. "Black hair, brown eyes, about four years old. Won't say his name."

"Noted. I'll investigate. Where are you now?" The voice crackled, but came back to full strength. What was that?

"Level nine section three," she replied.

"Okay, I can have someone meet you on level eight section six and she can take over the situation."

Juke could not contain her relief. "I owe you one, we'll be there."

Ending the call, she turned to Frida. The boy had stilled somewhat, but was nowhere near calm. "More stairs for us."

"My legs," Frida groaned.

"Don't they tell you not to skip leg day on Nox? Give him back to me and get back to work," Juke said.

"You know, I'm beginning to think this ship is worse than Nox," Frida replied wrestling the boy into Juke's arms.

"I'm inclined to agree."

They moved in silence, their lower quarters burning from the exertion. It had been hours. Why was it taking so long? "Frida?" Juke said, a shock running through her.

"Yeah?"

"Your dad, we can't move him. What can we do?" The idea of Frida's helpless dad being reduced to human rubble turned Juke's stomach, and her eyes stung with the knowledge of how the loss would affect Frida.

"I don't know, Juke. Maybe being in stasis will be enough to keep whatever it is from detecting him." She sighed, turning her focus back to her equations. "None of the possibilities are good."

"What do you mean?" Juke said as her struggling charge went limp and allowed himself to be carried.

Frida looked her in the eyes. "This thing… it could be a weapon, something to unleash on the other factions. Or some kind of predator. Maybe an alien entity that doesn't know it's hurting us?"

Juke shook her head. "It would have to know."

"Animals don't realize these things, some play. Take cats for instance, Like Pesky, they will play with mice, perhaps not realizing they're terrorizing them."

Juke tilted her head. "So you're suggesting a four dimensional animal is just having some fun?"

Frida shrugged. "It's just one theory."

They finally reached the stairs. Juke lead the way. They went slowly, their legs protesting every lift. Juke groaned as they reached the top, stumbling through the sliding doors before regaining her footing. Turning, she saw Frida struggling with every step, her face a mask of pain and determination. Juke slowed her pace so Frida could catch up, though doing so made her hands shake and goosebumps rise on her arms. "Come on Frida! We're almost there."

"Can't you have them adjust the gravity or something in here?"

Juke hadn't considered that. "I'll text Nin, maybe she's cooled down." Juke had her phone out, not answering. She fired off a quick text before putting it back in her pocket. "So—," she began, before being cut off by a voice from behind. A now familiar voice.

"Well, look who we have here. And a little friend, too. Hi little guy, it's good old uncle Lus."

Juke turned and glared. His fine suit was rumpled, but otherwise he was the same glorious bastard as ever. The child winced in Frida's arms.

Frida shook her head and tightened her grip. "What do you want, Lus? We're busy."

"Little guy looks like he weighs quite a bit. You both made quite the racket coming up the stairs. Let me take him," Lus said, meeting their pace.

"Fuck off old man," Frida said.

"See reason. You're both exhausted. I'm stronger than both of you, better able to sprint if need be." He cocked his head, his eyes boring into Juke's. "You see only the bad in me, I can assure you that I am capable of great good."

"You killed my mother," Frida spat at him.

"Ah, so Zeke finally told you. A pitiful, a sad accident back in my past," he said, hanging his head. "Yes, I am a monster of sorts, but I do not hurt children. Give me the boy," he ordered.

Frida tripped, almost going down onto her knees before being caught by Juke and Lus. "Okay, okay, you win," she said. "But, you owe me answers."

Lus took the boy from her arms, cradling him with ease. The boy squirmed but didn't put up much of a fight. "That wasn't so bad. Now ... what do you want to know?"

Chapter 25

Frida prepared herself mentally to question Lus. That hated creature. The monster of Dome-12. Security wasn't at the meeting location, so the three adults elected to do a loop of the seventh level. Juke pinged them on her phone, and waited for a reply. Frida's feet throbbed, each step becoming more painful than the last. The gravity had been decreased by about 25 percent, making the strain on her legs tolerable. Before she could open her mouth to ask why Lus needed power and control, why he was the way he was, her tablet buzzed.

"What was that?" Lus asked. They had been able to extract a name for the child—Potan. Not an uncommon one on Nox, but it was most popular generations ago.

"Maybe our way out of this mess," Frida said, activating the screen. She gasped. That was it.

"What is it?" Juke asked.

"I have it! I know where we need to go in this space!" Frida cried out, holding the tablet in front of her. "And you need to navigate, Juke."

"About damn time, can the *monkey* do it?" Lus asked, adjusting his load.

"Go fuck yourself, Lus. I need to get to the bridge. We can't do this with Potan," Juke said. "Only my console can steer the ship."

"Can't we call someone?" Frida asked. "Get someone closer? You can't be the only one who understands the helm."

Juke whipped out her phone, sending a message to Nin containing the coordinates and an explanation of what to do. "Okay, I just sent the coordinates out. Maybe someone else will be able to get there before we can."

"I suggest we get up there," Lus said.

"We have Potan, you can't carry him up seven flights of stairs. Not happening." Frida said. "You're not a young man."

"My dear, I am perfectly capable, and unlike you, I can afford longevity treatments. Now, do you want your answers or not?"

Frida slammed the side of her fist against the wall. "Fine."

"Don't let your anger get the better of you. Save your strength for the stairs," Lus said.

Frida fought down the urge to hit him, slap him across the face, punch him in the nose, kick him in the balls and leave him on the floor for the thing to find. The bastard was winning, and she knew it. "Was it you that put my father in that hospital bed?"

Lus laughed. It was a cold, chilling sound, like winter wind whistling over a weather vane. "I had nothing to do with that."

"Then why imply it?"

"Payback for my suit." Lus lovingly stroked Potan's hair as he pronounced each syllable. "You see, I don't like being rejected."

"And I don't like slimy old men," Frida shot back.

"Frida!" Juke interjected. "Both of you, calm down. We have no time for this bullshit. If I can't get to my console ..."

"Then someone else will do it, clearly you're replaceable," Lus said.

"How do you know about that?" Juke asked.

"So it is true," he replied.

They came to the stairs, and Frida took the lead, walking on the balls of her feet to adjust the weight she was placing on her feet. It was agonizing, but they had to get going. They exited onto level six. "I don't like this, something's not right," she said.

"Hate me all you like," Lus said.

"Shut up, it's not all about you. Why aren't we seeing people? The ship has dozens of people on board and all Juke and I have come across are the boy," Frida said, glancing at the pair.

Juke pulled out her phone. She'd received a message—a general order to all crew to report to the bridge and alter the ship's heading. "On the bright side, all crew are to report to the bridge. So if we don't make it, someone will."

"Someone." Frida felt a finality to the word. Who would save them? Or perhaps, the better question might be, should they start saving themselves. "We're going directly to the bridge, right now," she said. She knew that's what her father would do, and she was about to start following his example. Time to grow up.

"I thought we were meeting security to hand the boy over?" Lus asked.

Juke looked down at her phone. "I don't think they're coming."

Frida's mind recoiled at the thought. Were people simply starting to blink out of existence, rather than being smashed to death in this one? "Something isn't right."

"No shit," Lus said.

"Hey, language," Juke replied. "You're right, there are almost no acknowledgments to Nin's message. It's like the ship is being emptied."

"Come on, then, both of you. We gotta get Juke to the bridge," Frida said. "This fight can wait, we're alive now, and we need to stay that way."

Lus smiled, his face a death mask. "Truer words were never spoken."

***

"Can anyone hear me?" Juke spoke into her phone, changing channels and teams. Frida observed the lines on her face and bags under her eyes. Frida estimated that she looked every big as haggard. She hadn't slept or eaten well in days, and it was showing.

"Anyone?" They had already made it to level five, but their pace was flagging and they were becoming morose and passive by the minute. Frida couldn't find the will to fight with Lus, and likewise, he'd stopped antagonizing them. Being more than a century old, he likely had missed his afternoon nap. "Anyone? Respond."

"It's no use, either they're gone, they're in hiding, or something is interfering with the signal." Frida clamped her mouth shut after uttering the last possibility. There was no need to spread more fear and chaos than she already had.

"Hiding is a bad idea," Lus said.

"It makes sense if you're too tired to move," Juke groaned, lowering her phone. "It's like whatever this thing is means to wear us down."

"And force us to submit?" Frida asked.

"Think about it, Frida," Juke said. "It is the perfect weapon."

130

Lus chuckled. "She'd be right, Frida. If I had access to something like this half a century ago, all of Nox would be mine now."

"Disgusting."

"Just because you can't stomach what it takes to get ahead doesn't mean it's disgusting. Distasteful, perhaps, but you need a strong constitution to exist on Nox." Lus bobbed his head as he spoke.

"And I bet you loved every second of all you did to get where you are," Frida snapped.

"Did your father ever tell you what it was like before the Domes went up?" Lus asked, shifting his ward to his other hip.

"He was too young to remember much."

"Lus, leave her alone. She doesn't need to hear this," Juke said. "We're all in trouble, we need to work together."

"Men like me killed far fewer than the gangs that spawned from the festering pits after the Colonial Council collapsed. It took ten years, but Dome-12 is safe for children, women, and a haven for culture," Lus gloated. "All because of me."

"A damn hero," Frida muttered, her stomach churning. "What part did my mother play in your bloody grand plan?"

Lus sighed. "Chaos is a regrettable enemy. Now, there is order. Her sacrifice was not in vain."

Frida's vision tunneled, her hands balled into fists. "You bastard," she she spat. For her mother. For her father. For her own broken childhood. She took a step toward him, before Juke grabbed her, dragging her along by the shoulder.

"Not with Potan here, Frida. Not now, save your strength," Juke said softly.

"You heard what he said!"

"And I'll help you crush his shitty little skull later, but remember our mission. We need to live," Juke shook her with every word.

"Fine."

Frida seethed as they approached the stairs to level four. He was going to pay for her loss.

Chapter 26

The wind picked up just as they'd crossed the threshold to the fourth level. Their hair was whipped into a tornado-like frenzy. The presence was so powerful that it pressed against their lightened feet, threatening to throw them all into the ceiling at once. The hall was clear otherwise—it was just them. Juke looked at her traveling companions before letting loose a shout meant to command and inspire. "Run!"

Frida sped off ahead, paying no heed to where she was going. Juke and Lus followed closely, their panting breath lost in the turbulence. Potan began to scream, his shrieks echoing down the hall. Juke pushed harder—she had never been much of a runner, and her feet and legs were a testament to that now.

Lus gasped for air, his pace flagging. Longevity treatments or not, he was still an old man. "Let me take him, Lus!" Juke said.

"No," he wheezed.

A new scream resounded from further down the corridor. Frida had rolled her ankle, sending her careening into the right wall. She'd been knocked to her knees, and was scrambling to right herself. "Frida!" Juke shouted, pushing harder. Frida tried to stand, but fell again, and began crawling ahead in a desperate attempt to evade the inevitable.

"Go!" Frida said, waving her arm. "Go," she said, with tears beading in her eyes.

Before Juke could open her mouth to argue, the force of Potan being shoved into her arms caught her off-balance. Lus swooped into action, lifting Frida up and half-hauling, half-dragging her away. The boy struggled against Juke's grip, but she held fast, desperate to make it to Frida's side. "Come on!"

The wind slowed somewhat, the thing stilling itself. This time, the turbulence came from the other way, facing them. "What the hell?" Lus said.

"Shit," Juke said, unsure of how to approach this new situation. Was the thing toying with them like a cat with a mouse?

"Turn around," Frida gasped, leaning into Lus. Her right foot wasn't making contact with the floor and she held a death grip on Lus's shoulders.

They turned, heading back the way they came.

Then, the entity vanished, and the wind stilled. It was just them, their desperate need for air, and the terror that was left in its wake.

"Oh, hells," Frida groaned. Her breaths came in short gasps, wheezing with every labored inhalation.

"I got you, uncle Lus is here," Lus said. "I told you, I protect."

Frida hung her head and carried on hopping on her one good foot.

Juke looked at Potan. "Hey little guy, can you walk for a bit?" she asked. With a sniffle, he nodded. Juke put him down. "Hold onto my hand and do not let go, ever. Okay?" Potan toddled along, rubbing his eyes and snotty wet nose. Juke didn't want to be the one to clean him up once they got to safety. She was not gifted with kids. "How are you doing, Frida?"

"I can't use my foot," she said. "I may have broken my ankle."

Juke's hand went to her forehead—this was bad. "Shit," Juke said. "Can you keep going?"

"Have to," Frida grunted.

"Let's get to the stairs before the thing comes back," Lus suggested.

"Yeah, let's do that," Juke replied.

Juke walked in silence, taking the opportunity to check her phone and attempt to contact someone—anyone. There were two or three acknowledgments and pledges to reach the bridge, but with a crew of 15, that seemed like a very small list. She wondered if the engineers were hiding out somewhere—Branx was a known coward. She'd seen him run from more fights on shore leave than there were moons on Antares II. His staff were equally craven. She estimated he didn't want to employ anyone who could take him in a fight. A new message pinged her phone —Nin was on her way to the bridge. Juke sighed. Good and bad news. Hopefully, she would beat them there and do what needed to be done.

"Anyone else feel like the walls are narrower?" Lus asked.

"That's just because you're standing so close," Frida replied.

"A sense of humor can help in these kinds of situations, I'm glad you're feeling better Frida," Lus said, straightening suddenly.

Frida grunted, re-aligning herself on her good leg. Juke's teeth clenched. She really was going to kill him when they were done, and blame it on an accident.

"Ow!" Potan cried out.

"Sorry!" Juke said, realizing she had squeezed his small hand too tightly.

When they finally reached the stairs to the third level. Frida winced. "This is gonna suck."

"You can always crawl," Lus suggested.

Frida seemed to process that for a moment. "Fine, but you're going up first."

"Why?"

"I don't want you gawking at me, crawling in front of you," she replied.

Juke sighed. Why did it have to be Lus they ran into? The dick was complicating things. Juke never wanted to see or hear about Nox-Gamma ever again if it meant having him as a passenger.

"I see." Lus took off up the stairs, leaving Frida on all-fours, picking her along, wincing with every contact of her knees on metal.

Juke followed Frida, coaxing Potan. His presence was a definite hindrance, but at least he'd calmed down enough to give her ears a break. "Come on, Frida, you got this," Juke whispered. "You're so strong, so smart, you mean so much to me."

Frida turned her head back and gave a half-smile. "Oh come on, Juke."

Juke smiled, in spite of everything. Frida, though, was exceptional. Special, and there was a magic to her that sprung itself on Juke, making her feel for the first time in years. Yes, it could be love. Lus tutted from ahead, but Juke didn't care. That old monster couldn't change reality. Juke smiled. As terrible as things were, with Frida here, it wasn't so bad. They would weather it together.

They came onto the third level, and Lus helped Juke haul Frida back to an upright position They had to start moving again. Juke was starting to hate this ship, which stunned her. Having lived here for eleven years, at some point that she'd come to believe that she never wanted to leave. "You know, at one time I thought this would be my home forever," she said out loud.

"What changed?" Frida asked.

"Time changed me. I started here when I was fresh out of school. Didn't know anything. Didn't want to stay home, just wanted to see the galaxy."

"Maybe you should have joined the army," Lus said. "They see a lot more."

"I'm a pacifist, but for you I'd make an exception," she replied.

"I see."

"Why now? Was it because of me?" Frida said.

"In part, yeah. I'd already been thinking of doing something else, but I realized I've been trying so long to fit in on a ship where I'm not even accepted. Branx is nasty, Nin can't stand me. Why am I putting up with this, right?" Juke replied, the words finally giving her thoughts life.

"Yeah, I get it. I need a change, too," Frida said.

Lus muttered something under his breath.

"You still want to check out the museums on planet with me? I'm no expert, but I can offer a tour. I can find my way around those places with my eyes closed." Juke let herself smile. A future, any future, was something to cling to. And cling she did, needing the warm glow of hope to compel her aching body to move on, to keep Potan under control, and to put up with Lus.

"I'd love to, Juke. Anywhere with you, anytime." Frida struggled to support herself on both feet, and checked her tablet. "We need to speed up, we're losing time. If we're the last ones going for the bridge, then we gotta save ourselves. We can't count on anyone else. And I want to see the sun for the first time in my life."

"It's overrated," Lus interjected.

"You'd say and do anything to keep me on Nox," Frida barked.

"I obviously can't stop you from leaving, but I can make it worth your while to stay," he said.

"Don't care. It's worth your while to shut up."

"Everyone comes back, you know. Nox is comfortable. You'll feel like you're falling into the sky the first time you see it. The moon will keep you awake at night. Rain will ruin your hair. Think of it, none of those things exist back home, it's controlled and predictable. I suspect you like things that way, Frida," Lus concluded, stretching himself to his full height and rolling his shoulders.

"Let me worry about falling into the sky, I know more about gravity than you ever will," Frida replied.

Get him, girl, Juke thought. That was the woman she had come to love. These past few days have cultivated her, changed her from a bookworm to someone engaged with life. Juke had discovered a transformation in herself as well. It was what she needed. "We're almost there, let's go get this done," she said, her tone one of command. Frida wasn't going down without a fight, and neither was she.

Chapter 27

"We're at the bridge!" Juke announced, bringing a smile to Frida's face. It was dark. They'd passed some unlucky passengers, ill-fated humans on the last few floors, but no living people were to be seen. Potan was back in her arms. He was squirming, and Juke was whispering calming words to him. If only he would fall asleep, things would be far less complicated. Her ankle throbbed and stabbed with every step, but her resolve held fast. So close, so close, was her mantra. Nothing else mattered, not Lus, not her trip away from Nox. They got Juke to the bridge, mission accomplished.

"Get us in," Lus said.

Juke placed her hand against the scanner in the rectangular panel next to the door. While she did this, Lus and Frida walked in circles in the antechamber. Frida didn't take her eyes off Juke, who was standing still. Frida's stomach lurched. "Hurry, Juke!" she called out. "You can't stand still, remember!"

The door slid open, admitting them to the bridge. Juke rushed in and cursed. Frida's mouth fell open. The bridge was a mass of blood, the stench overwhelming. "Oh, hells," Lus said. "Stay outside with the kid, Frida. I'm going in."

Frida wasn't about to argue. "What are you going to do in that mess?"

"Look for survivors," he replied. "I've seen worse."

I bet you have. Frida continued limping, dragging Potan in long, random paths around the anteroom, trying not to repeat a route more than once. Her ankle throbbed, but she grit her teeth and forced herself to move.

"I'm there!" Juke yelled. "Plotting a new course should only take a minute," she added.

"But you're standing still!" Frida shouted back.

"I have to do this, Frida. It's the only way." Beeping and button presses could be heard from the console. "Looks like someone started but wasn't able to finish."

"I'll cover her, Frida," Lus said, adding: "There's no one left alive here."

"What?" Frida shouted. "Lus, you're actually going to protect something?"

"You heard me. Keep Potan out of trouble, and listen to old uncle Lus for once."

Just then, the stillness of the air transformed into a gale. Droplets of blood and human remains began rising up from the floor. "No!" Juke shouted. "No, no, no!" Potan began sobbing as the familiar presence filled Frida's body, threatening to overcome her senses and make her stop dead in her tracks. Frida redoubled her efforts and pushed on, her terror and anger were all that was powering her battle against the unknown force.

Juke screamed. Frida rushed to the door of the bridge, almost freezing in her tracks at the sight. Juke's signature ponytail was standing straight up, and she clung to the console with her left hand as her right hand worked the controls. Frida couldn't see Juke's eyes, but her mouth was an array of white teeth, clenched and strained. Her legs were hooked around her bench. There was nowhere to run, nowhere for her to hide.

"Juke!" Frida shouted. Juke was their only hope, and she was about to be wiped out by that killing machine. That hunter-thing that seemed to live on human blood.

Lus looked at Frida. "I got this," he said, charging towards Juke's station. His movement had speed and grace that defied his advanced age. He leapt onto the console's bench, holding Juke down. But, it was a futile gesture. Lus was picked up by the slow pull of the anti-gravity monster. It spun him, the rotations gathering speed. Juke looked up, hit three more buttons and dove under her console.

Lus's end was as violent as his life. His head connected with the bulkhead of the bridge's ceiling, an audible crack sounding across the room, Frida rushed Potan away from the door, making sure he couldn't see the gory scene playing out before them. The wind stopped, the presence faded. A thud was heard as what was left of Lus's body collided with the floor. Frida emptied her stomach, unable to keep moving for that brief moment while her body rejected the horror of the past few day's experiences.

"Juke?" she called out. "Juke, are you okay?"

"Yes, thanks to Lus." Juke pulled herself out from under her console, her clothes splattered in blood. "It's done."

Aesop's impassive voice interrupted: "Attention all hands, we are moving away from the anomaly. We will be clear in approximately 106 minutes. Continue moving until told otherwise."

"Approximately? Let's get out of here," Frida said, as they moved towards the stairs. "Maybe we can just limit our roaming to level one?"

"I programmed a distress call to begin as soon as we reach clear space," Juke said, following behind. "We can't lose our rescuers, too."

"Juke?"

"Yes?"

"Why did Lus sacrifice himself?" Frida asked.

"I think he had a revelation about the value his life held. Evidently, you got under his skin. I really don't know." Juke offered, taking Frida's hand. "The point is, he did, and for that we should be grateful."

Frida remained silent for a moment, contemplating this. She and Juke had had similar realizations recently. Could it be possible that even a monster like Lus could reflect? "Well, I'm glad you are still here."

"Me, too, trust me. Let me tell everyone it's done." Juke pulled out her phone, and sent an alert to the crew that the course had been changed and they were on their way to safety. "We'll be safe soon. We were actually close to your coordinates, Frida," she said.

"Hey!" a voice shouted behind them. "You're alive!" Frida could place the voice. But, she didn't know from where. Footfalls were closing in on them fast.

 Frida turned to face the sound. "Glizzy!"

Juke laughed. "How did you manage to survive all this time?"

Glizzy cleared their throat. "I might be a simple bartender, but I'm not stupid. When everyone decided to hide, I listened to the damn captain and danced around my damn bar. No rum required."

"I'm glad to see you, Glizzy," Juke said.

"Me too," Frida offered.

"Can we stop moving yet?" they asked.

"Not yet, Aesop will tell us. Give it an hour or two," Juke replied.

"Where are we going, after we clear this space?" Frida asked.

"We're still heading to Elym, don't worry. I expect we'll get evacuated; the ship is in no condition to get there under without its crew," Juke replied.

"Have you encountered anyone else?" Glizzy asked.

Frida explained their time with Lus, and his final act, one not of greed, but of heroism.

"The hells? That creep, sacrificed himself for the flight monkey?" Glizzy exclaimed.

"I'm right here, I can hear you damn it," Juke said, as they moved down the hall.

Glizzy scooped Potan into their arms, cooing at the child "I just can't believe it. I'll never serve black coffee again to Lus again! And we'll get you to the daycare, yes we will," they added, turning their affections to Potan.

Frida looked down, seeing the blood-crusted trim on her pants, and her ruined shoes clinging to her skin. The knots in her stomach and the weakness of her limbs complimented her ruined clothes. Her body demanded rest, but rest, she hoped, would come soon enough.

"So tell me, are you two a couple? The rumors have been circulating for days. Probably the last juicy piece of gossip on the ship," Glizzy said.

Frida and Juke looked at each other and smiled. Frida squeezed Juke's hand. "Yes," they said in unison.

Glizzy simply clapped. Frida didn't know what else to say. Instead she concentrated on the next step. The next hall. The next section. Always the next thing, until they were free from the existential threat of the mysterious presence.

Chapter 28

Three chimes sounded. Then came a repeat. The lights in the corridor of level one section three flashed red and white. "Emergency alert terminated. Return to your quarters." Aesop's voice spoke, it was both commanding and tinny. Juke's face lit up. It was over. They were safe. She sighed and pulled Frida in close. "We did it," she whispered.

"No, you did it," Frida replied. "You saved us all."

"Would you accept 'We make a great team'?" Juke squeezed harder before letting go.

"I might, if the time frame tends to infinity."

Glizzy looked at them both. "I can tell you two need to be alone, how about I take Potan to the daycare lounge and let you both get some rest?"

"What do you know about kids?" Juke asked.

"Probably more than you both do. Big family, you know," Glizzy responded. "Hopefully the kid's palace is clean, I can't very well take the little guy to the bar."

"Fair enough," Juke said as Glizzy scooped Potan up in their arms and carried him off.

Frida groaned. "I need some sleep. And fresh clothes. And a memory wipe."

"My quarters are closest, let's go." Juke winked.

"I don't think I'm up for much excitement," Frida said, a yawn cracking her jaw. "I need sleep and to check in on dad."

"Then sleep you shall get, after we visit sickbay. I need to stay awake to respond to the rescue, but you go ahead."

Frida smiled. "You sure?"

"I'll be right there with you. No nightmares tonight, promise." She moved in close, helping Frida support her hurt ankle. "I have you."

"Juke?"

"Thank you, for everything."

***

Sickbay was silent, the too-bright lights glaring over every surface. The staff was nowhere to be found. Juke skimmed the beds at the back of the room, ignoring everything else. Frida clung to her shoulder, hanging like a dead weight. Juke's feet and legs ached, but she didn't care.

"Dad!" Frida shouted out, stumbling towards his bed.

Juke smiled. There he lay, shimmering yellow force field still intact. Stasis must have protected him, somehow. Juke walked to his side, looking down at him. He was deathly still, but whole. The machine still worked its magic in keeping him alive. "He's okay," she breathed.

"Dad...," Frida choked, pressing a hand against the dancing light.

"He's going to be okay, Frida. Let's get you to bed," Juke said.

"But...," Frida began. "He's all alone."

"And he'll be awake before you know it. Come on." Juke placed a hand on Frida's shoulder.

Frida looked long and hard at Zeke before turning away. "Okay, I'm ready."

***

Juke sat at her console, shaking a bottle of stimulants while her feet were propped on the desk, boots off. She contemplated taking yet another. Did her duty mean more than her health? She could access most of the ship's systems from her quarters, and answer the comms. She leaned back, basking in the ecstasy of a seated position. The drugs made everything feel amazing, even her feet. She closed her eyes, and listened to the sounds of Frida's heavy breathing from the bedroom. She was fast asleep. Juke longed to go to her and hold her close, but she had to keep Frida, Glizzy, Potan, and any other survivors safe. *I wonder if Zeke is still okay*, she thought. Juke knew Frida would shatter into a million pieces if she lost him. Setting the bottle back on the desk, she took a swig of cold coffee, making a face as it hit her tongue. How Lus had tolerated this stuff was beyond her comprehension, but it did have a certain appeal to it.

Frida began snoring. Juke found it adorable. Turning up the volume on her monitor, she pushed her chair back and stood. Gingerly, she made her way to the bed and sat down next to Frida, simply watching. This whole adventure was a fight for survival, and there they were. Together. Frida had been asleep for about six hours at this point. Juke resolved not to waken her, so back to her desk she went. Easing down, she scanned for ships, signals, anything. Was anyone coming to help them?

It was an inane question. The Council placed great importance on the intrinsic value of human life. They'd come, even for one person. She just had to be patient. She picked up a book from her desk, one that held images of an ancient Earth museum long since destroyed by war, its masterpieces melted in nuclear fire. As she flipped the pages, the beauty of a moment came to her in a burst of realization. Nothing lasts. Each image, the product of untold hours of creation, destroyed by some senseless war over ideology. Humanity could create, yes, but they were infinitely more gifted at destruction.

Setting the book down, Juke opened the data banks on her console. She loaded the files on basic mathematical theory. It was time to see into Frida's world. If Juke could introduce Frida to the wonders of art, then she could appreciate a theorem or two. It was only fair.

***

The console beeped, startling Juke. She had been staring at the ceiling, contemplating the similarities between math and art. Perhaps they were the same? Some mathematical constructs very much resembled abstract art. She turned to the monitor, and smiled. It was a hail! She quickly answered.

"This is Helmsman Juke Frin of the cargo ship Destiny."

"I am Captain Kel Hun of the rescue ship Excelsior. How can we assist you?"

Juke explained the story in its gory entirety. Hun's face fell as she continued, appearing to be equal parts ill and confused. Juke could detect an element of green creeping into his skin. "Can you remotely stop the ship and dock?" she asked at the end. Some rescue ships could.

"Yes, yes of course. Where is your captain?"

"Unknown, sir."

"Very well. I am assuming command. You look like hell, get some rest."

"Yes, sir."

With that, the screen winked out, leaving only the computer's dashboard and meters on display. Juke pulled herself to her feet and groaned. She let down her hair, feeling it tumble over her shoulders. Stripping out of her bloody pants and shirt, she crawled into bed next to Frida, holding her tight. Frida stirred, but did not wake. Juke knew the stimulants wouldn't let her sleep, but this would be rest enough. Closing her eyes, she focused on Frida's breathing. Was this really what she'd been missing all these years? A sense of closeness to another human being?

Chapter 29

Frida and Juke walked hand in hand down the corridor, past the rescue and cleanup crews towards the medical bay. The air was laden with the scent of chemical cleaners, and voices carried down the halls, giving the illusion that the ship was speaking to them. Sometimes the voices cursed or cried out. Frida hoped they weren't adding vomit to the already putrid mess that was the ship's decks. They'd probably seen worse, by virtue of their chosen line of work.

Walking into sickbay, Frida shrieked and ran to Zeke's side. She tried to hug him, but was repelled by the zap and spray of the yellow force field. Frida's cheeks reddened as Juke laughed.

"You'd hug him, too!" Frida said.

"I'll wait until there are no shocks involved," Juke replied.

"Fair."

Frida examined her father, his closed eyes, pallid complexion and still chest all gave the illusion of death. But, she knew he was alive. However, the tears came to her eyes and she turned away from him, burying her face in Juke's shoulder. Strong arms wrapped around her, and there they stood for what seemed an eternity.

"Miss Juniper?" a woman's voice queried.

Frida jumped. "Yes?"

"We're going to move him now, do you want to accompany him or will you leave the ship later?"

Frida looked up at Juke and smiled. "Can we go now?"

Juke's grip on her was released, and they walked across the room as two medics prepared the anti-grav stretcher. With that and a distinct humming sound, Zeke's bed floated out of the room. Frida and Juke followed closely, not wanting to lose sight of him. They had already made arrangements to have their belongings moved, and Juke had filed her resignation from the cargo company that owned the Destiny. Now, the future was up to them.

***

"Welcome to the Excelsior," Captain Hun said as they crossed the threshold. There were a few passengers Frida recognized milling about the loading bay, but none acknowledged her. Potan and Glizzy were nowhere to be seen, but Nin was standing in the corner absorbed in her tablet, her back to the room. A small cat carrier sat next to her, and Pesky was yowling incessantly. It was a large chamber, with a tall ceiling and bright lights. Compared to the Destiny, this was luxurious. Frida stayed close to Juke, her stomach tied in knots, as all kinds of situations playing in her head. She wondered if they'd ask how she figured it out. If she was in league with the thing. If it spared her on purpose. She sucked in a deep breath and tried to steady herself. She'd let Juke do the talking.

"Thank you, Captain Hun," Juke replied.

"I understand you'll be rooming together for the trip back?" he asked.

"Yes, sir," Juke said, grinning.

"Very well. You're assigned to level fifteen cabin eight. Contact the custodians should you require anything." He shot Frida a hard look, and turned away.

"One question," Juke said.

"Make it quick."

"Where did you find Captain Nin?" she asked.

"Under her desk in the office. Seems she can't handle the sight of blood," replied Hun.

"Thank you, sir. Let's go, Frida" Juke said.

They walked down the corridor, which was wide and white, with floor panels that lit up as they were stepped on. There was no hum like on the Destiny, and the air was fresh and clean. Frida counted up the levels as they passed, until they'd reached level fifteen. Rushing, they flung themselves down the hall, with no reservation or concern for who might see them or whatever safety rules existed. They were safe. Juke was free.

They came to their quarters, and she pressed her hand to the locking panel. The door slid open without a sound, revealing a small but plush room. There was a sofa that looked like it belonged to the richest families on Nox, a bed with many pillows, its own gleaming lavatory and panel windows that gave the most perfect view of the stars. Frida smiled. "It's perfect, Juke," she said.

They stepped inside and fell onto the couch. "I could stay here forever, with you," Juke said.

"No way."

"What?" Juke startled and turned to face her.

"You're taking me to the museum, remember?"

The chamber rang with their laughter as the Excalibur got underway. There was much to heal, but time and care would see to that.

Chapter 30

Juke stood behind Frida. They were in the main hospital on Elym-One, a grandiose building of lights and beige tones. They both had their eyes on Zeke, watching the color return to his face, his breathing resume, his eyes flutter. It took minutes, hours, but they sat down and continued to watch with rapt attention. Frida reached out and held his hand, squeezing it periodically. "He's getting warmer," she said.

"Good, he'll be back with us soon," Juke said.

"And just in time, the conference is starting in two days and I'm not even ready! I need to practice, I need to memorize my talking points, I ..."

Juke grabbed her by the shoulders. "You need to relax. You'll make us both proud."

Frida turned. "You're going?"

Juke grinned. "I've been studying. I wouldn't miss it for all the colonies in the Confederation."

"Studying?"

"Yeah. I figured if you want to see my world, it's only fair that I should see yours."

"Juke, I—," Frida began.

Zeke stirred, his eyes fluttering open. He muttered something before tumbling back into his artificial slumber.

"Did you see that, Frida? Everything is going to be okay. Trust me."

Frida smiled. "Even my speech?"

"Yes, even your speech."

***

Zeke was sitting up in his bed, being checked out by a doctor who had to be at least two centuries old. How the doctor was still willing to work at that age was unfathomable to Juke, but hells, she was only thirty one. What did she know? Frida stood at his side, but Juke didn't feel comfortable listening in on their private conversation, so she watched from a distance. Therapy was scheduled for later that day, and she badly needed it. Nightmares wouldn't let her sleep, and so much as the touch of a breeze would set her off running. It was going to be difficult to transition to life on the planet side, but she was up for the challenge.

Frida turned away from her father and the doctor, smiling. As she walked over, she was neat and proper, just as she had been that first day when she'd boarded the Destiny. So unlike the exhausted and terrified young woman back on the ship. They left the room, and walked towards the exit. "Are you ready to fall into the sky?" Juke asked.

Frida looked at her for a moment, then her eyes opened wide. "If you're with me, I'm ready for anything."

"Trust me, you can take care of yourself," Juke replied. "You don't need protection."

Frida fell silent for a moment. "Why did Lus do it?" she asked.

"Save me?" Juke replied.

"Yeah. He'd been a self-serving bastard for decades. Why would he sacrifice himself?"

"Sometimes, seeing things like that changes a person. Maybe he realized there were things his money couldn't buy. Maybe he heard we were going to a museum and realized he wasn't invited. Honestly, I don't know." Juke paused and checked the signs on the ceiling to make sure they were still heading for the exit. "What does matter is we're safe. You get to do your presentation, then we can figure out how to stay on Elym-One."

"When you put it that way—"

"Believe in yourself. You're stronger than you think. How's your dad?"

"He'll be out in time for the conference."

"Excellent, I'm glad." Juke smiled. It really was good news. She was happy Zeke had been spared the worst of the horrors. He'd had seen enough in his lifetime, he didn't need an hours-long death march added to his personal experience. "Think he'd be up for a museum trip?"

"I'm not sure. We'll take it as it goes," Frida said.

They came to the exit, and Frida hesitated as she grasped the handle of the double doors. Then she flung it open, and stepped into the sunlight. Her hand rushed to cover her eyes, and she stumbled to a halt. Juke grabbed her. "I got you," she said. Frida lowered her hand, squinting.

"It's so bright, and it's hot, it really is hot!" she said.

"That's the sun, it was night when we arrived, remember?"

"Yeah," Frida said, looking up. "The sky is so blue, and ... are those clouds?" She pointed upwards.

Juke followed her finger to a poofy cumulus cloud. "Yup. That's a cloud. You'll see a lot of them out here in the real world."

"I want to see more," Frida said.

"Come with me," Juke replied.

Epilogue

Frida sat with Zeke outside their new home—a small white cottage with a flat roof on the outskirts of Hisak, Elym-One's capital city. There was a tree in the front yard, covered in red and white blossoms, whose fragrance was so sweet it could be tasted —a milblossom tree, she'd been told. Frida had insisted on this house because of that tree, and Juke had happily obliged. She rocked in her chair, enjoying the squeaking it made every time it came forward. She watched the sky, counting clouds, occasionally pointing out a new one with an interesting shape to Zeke. He'd chuckle and go back to his reading.

She pulled out her tablet, the same one that she'd used to save the Destiny weeks ago, and went back to scouring the city for jobs ads. It was difficult to decide where to go, when so many options were open to her.

Juke walked off the street, plunking herself down in an empty chair. By comparison, she'd found work very easily and quickly. Seems everyone wanted to have the hero of the Molorus sectoro as their designer. "Hello there!"

Frida waved and returned to her search.

A car stopped in front of their home, its purring engine melting into the dull background ambiance of the city. Footsteps approached. A voice cleared. "Frida Juniper?"

Frida started and moved her gaze upwards. Two men stood in front of them, both wearing suits. One with spiky red hair stood with his hands on his hips, the other with a crooked nose and longer black hair had his arms crossed.

"Yes?" Juke and Zeke were scrutinizing them, too.

"It came to our attention that you are seeking employment, is that the case?" said the man with his hands on his hips.

"Who are you, and why do you ask?"

"I'm Drin," said the man on the left, removing his hands from his hips. "This is Swi," he pointed to the other man. He nodded. "We're from the Confederacy Council."

Frida stopped to consider. Jobs with the Council were almost unheard of, and never advertised. "What kind of job?" she asked.

"Your efforts on board the Destiny did not go unnoticed. We would like your expertise, to help enable us to detect and even perhaps control, these anomalies."

Frida's mouth fell open. "Control?"

"It's better for all involved if we're able to keep our ships safe, no?" He shrugged. "You'll find that the work is rewarding and the pay is good. Perhaps we can step inside your house and discuss the finer points of our offer there?"

Frida glanced at Juke and Zeke. They wore expressions that were blank and noncommittal, but their arms were crossed in a protective position. Juke stood. "I think Zeke and I should join you."

"This is confidential, between us and Miss Juniper," Drin said.

"I want them with me," Frida said.

"You want them involved in confidential matters?" Drin asked.

"There is nothing I'd like more than to keep my loved ones close," Frida shot back.

Drin motioned towards the door. "Then, let us begin."

Frida took one last look at the sky before walking into her home, followed by Zeke and Juke. She didn't know what was happening.

Time would tell if the Council's offer would be a boon or bane.

Thea Gregory is a science fiction and fantasy author. When she's not crafting her multiverses, she enjoys daydreaming, gardening, and many kinds of video games. Her creative process is often accompanied by her mischievous cat, Bonk, who occasionally disrupts her flow. She resides in the Montreal area with her partner and, of course, Bonk.

Did you enjoy *n-Space*? Please consider helping me out by leaving an honest review.

Sign up for my monthly newsletter and receive a free short story set in the *Worshipers of the Black Hole*'s universe. Download *Singular Truth* here:

https://planetthea.com/free-story/

For more of my work, including *Worshipers of the Black Hole*, the *Zombie Bedtime Stories*, and *The ABACUS Protocol* series, join my newsletter or follow my social media:

Website: https://planetthea.com
Threads: @author.thea.g
Instagram: @author.thea.g
Facebook group:
https://www.facebook.com/groups/TheaGregory
https://www.facebook.com/TheaIsisGregory/